TAKE A CHANCE ON ME

A marathon brings doctors Anna Curtis and Riordan 'Mac' McKenna together. Anna has moved into the area with her late sister's little boy, Cameron, and Mac offers her a job at his surgery. They become close and Anna falls pregnant. However, when Mac's ex-wife informs her that he doesn't want children, she decides she must move away. Can Mac finally convince her that he loves her, Cameron and the baby?

TERESA ASHBY

TAKE A CHANCE ON ME

Complete and Unabridged

LINFORD
Leicester

First published in Great Britain in 2010

First Linford Edition
published 2012

British Library CIP Data

Ashby, Teresa.
  Take a chance on me - -
  (Linford romance library)
  1. Love stories.
  2. Large type books.
  I. Title II. Series
  823.9′2–dc23

  ISBN 978–1–4448–1178–0

Published by
F. A. Thorpe (Publishing)
Anstey, Leicestershire

Set by Words & Graphics Ltd.
Anstey, Leicestershire
Printed and bound in Great Britain by
T. J. International Ltd., Padstow, Cornwall

This book is printed on acid-free paper

1

Anna had been ignoring the gnawing ache in her foot for the past mile or so, but now the pain was almost unbearable.

One more thump of her foot on the hot, hard road and it was too much, she stumbled forwards, palms grazing on the ground.

Tears of anger and frustration gathered behind her closed lids as she tried to get back to her feet and failed. She was dimly aware of people coming to her aid, hands reaching out to help her to her feet.

It was so infuriating. She'd hit the wall some time ago, run through it and knew she had enough energy to finish. If only her stupid foot hadn't let her down. She'd trained properly, was as prepared as she could be and yet with the end almost in sight her feet had been knocked from under her.

She shook the hands from her arms and with a huge determined effort made it back onto her feet. But putting weight on that painful foot was so hard and there were still two miles to go to the end.

'I have to finish this,' she said, jutting out her chin determinedly. 'I have to do it for Christa.'

She took a step forward and winced. Her whole body shook, pain and exertion made her sweat, but she hadn't just run 24 miles to give up now.

An arm went round her waist and she felt herself being bunched up against a solid wall of muscle. She was about to pull free, thinking it was someone else trying to pull her out of the marathon, but the guy who smiled down at her was another competitor. She'd noticed him at the start.

His face was tanned which made his piercing pale blue eyes look all the more striking. His short, dark hair was damp and flat against his head and his smile was absolutely devastating. If Anna hadn't already had a wobble in her legs, she was sure her knees would have buckled anyway.

'I've got to finish,' she said fiercely as if this total stranger might even begin to understand. 'For Christa.'

'I know,' he said and when she gave him a questioning look he smiled again. 'It's on your T-shirt and it's a great cause. Aplastic anaemia.'

'It killed my sister,' she said huskily. 'Who are you running for?'

'Motor neurone,' he said. 'Lean on me . . . Keep the weight off that foot.'

She looked up at him, hope flaring inside her. She had never liked accepting help from anyone. From an early age she'd learned that the only person you could rely on was yourself. She had to swallow her pride and accept the help that was offered. But she didn't want to ruin someone else's chances and he'd looked to her as though he was running to win.

'Are you sure? I'll slow you down . . . '

'I'm not racing,' he said easily. 'As long as I get across the line it doesn't matter when I finish.'

'I don't even know your name,' she said as they set off with him taking most of her weight.

'Riordan McKenna but everyone calls me Mac,' he said, his voice normal, as if helping Anna required no physical effort whatsoever. 'I'm part of the team running for the Grange Road Family Practice.'

'You're a doctor?'

'Currently *the* doctor,' he said ruefully. 'I've been running the practice on locums and good hope for the past few months with occasional help from my father. How about you?'

'Anna Curtis,' she said. 'If you're a doctor should you be encouraging me to keep moving?'

'Would you take any notice if I told you to keep off the foot and seek medical attention?' He grinned.

'No.' She smiled, deliberately not mentioning the fact that she was pretty sure that bones had fractured. If she admitted that, then he was sure to make her stop.

'What else?' he asked, tightening his grip around her waist and holding her against him. 'There must be more to Anna Curtis than an injured foot.'

Breathless and occasionally gasping with pain was no way to carry on a getting-to-know you conversation.

And just how did a man who had just run over twenty miles smell so good, she wondered? Not quite as if he'd just stepped out of a shower, but not far from it.

Someone pounded past.

'Hey, Mac,' he called. 'I hope you've brought your wallet with you — I'd prefer cash, but I'll accept a cheque if you don't have it on you.'

'Very funny. We could use a hand here, Martin,' Mac said.

The other runner turned and jogged backwards so he was facing them. Anna didn't like the triumphant sneer on his face.

'Looks as if you're handling things well on your own, Mac.' He laughed. 'I wouldn't want to cramp your style.'

'Don't worry,' Mac said. 'I'll still cross the line before you.'

The other guy roared with laughter, then turned and ran ahead. He wasn't going very fast, but he could have walked and still moved faster than Mac and Anna.

'Leave me,' she said, outraged on Mac's behalf. 'You can't let him beat you, not after that.'

'He won't beat me,' Mac grinned. 'Believe me — it's the hare and the tortoise all over again. He'll be so busy congratulating himself and playing up to any girls that might be watching he won't even see us sneak past.'

'You sound very sure,' she said wryly.

'I am. He's my cousin and we grew up together. I know him too well.'

Anna picked up her pace, hopping furiously. She wanted Mac to beat his cousin. They covered quite a distance like that, but her good leg was beginning to ache and Mac seemed to be tiring, too.

'This won't do,' he said at last. 'It isn't working like this. We can't carry on. You're going to wear your other foot out and I'm going to end up walking round lop-sided for the rest of my life.'

'I'm sorry,' she said with genuine regret. Not just that she was about to be left on her own, but because she liked his company and would be truly sorry to see his back vanishing into the distance. But there was a bright side. She had no doubt he would speed away and overtake his cousin. He let go of her, then turned his back.

'Come on,' he said, smiling over his shoulder.

'What?'

He held his arms out at his sides and looked over his shoulder at her.

'You're what, twenty-five? Not that long since you were a kid. I bet you did this with your dad.' When she still looked at him, puzzled, he continued. 'Piggyback. Put your arms round my neck and I'll do the rest.'

'You've got to be joking.' She laughed. 'You'll never manage to run the final two miles with me on your back — I'll only begin to weigh you down!'

'Well, we can try,' he said. 'Come on. You don't look that heavy.'

'I'm not twenty-five,' she added. 'Nearer to thirty, but thanks anyway.'

And I never had a dad to give me piggybacks, either, she added silently.

As Anna reached up, he curled his arms back and under her bottom, lifting her effortlessly until she could wrap her legs around his middle.

The onlookers cheered from the pavement and Anna waved to them.

Look, Christa, she thought. *I'm going to make it after all.*

There were hundreds of runners, but Mac's eyes had found her in the crowd at the start. He'd already decided to focus on someone in front rather than at the ground before his feet and, lucky him, he'd chosen Anna.

She wasn't fast, but she was powerful for someone of such a slim build and he'd found the back view of her fascinating, from her little pointed elbows flashing back and forth to her tiny waist and those shapely legs.

Further up she had a slim, straight neck and her long, fair hair was caught back in a high ponytail that swung from side to side as she ran. He'd even slowed his own pace so he could keep behind her, keep her in his sights.

He told himself it was a matter of self preservation. He might just as easily have chosen the guy dressed as a clown or the woman running for an animal charity with the little toy dog peeking out of a knapsack on her back to focus on, but he hadn't.

And then her stride had started to fail. She was favouring one foot over the other until it became a limp and then suddenly a fall. He'd almost run into the back of her and would have agreed with everyone else that her race should end right there, but for the plaintive sound of her voice when she said she had to keep going for Christa. He had no doubt that she would crawl along the rest of the way on her hands and knees if she had to and in that case she'd end up with skinned knees as well as a sprained ankle — or whatever her injury was.

He wondered how long ago Anna had lost her sister to aplastic anaemia. Not long if the dark shadow of sadness that lingered in her eyes or the ferocity of her determination was anything to go by. She had the look of a person who had recently suffered great loss and the purpose of someone desperate to achieve something to compensate for that loss.

As he predicted they passed his cousin who had slowed his pace so he could jog beside a couple of pretty girls in extremely short shorts and very tight tops. He was so engrossed that he didn't even see Mac pass by with Anna on his back. Mac heard Anna's soft laugh and smiled. Beating Martin to the finish was going to be sweet.

After a while she seemed heavier. Her breath in his ear was hot.

'Put me down, Mac,' she urged him several times. 'This isn't fair. You'll exhaust yourself . . . Hurt your back . . .'

'Shut up, woman,' he gently growled back at her and she laughed softly.

He picked up his pace and turned his thoughts towards next week when the latest in a long line of locums was due to start at the practice. The patients were fed up with it and all were asking for appointments with him rather than see an unfamiliar face. His workload was becoming unbearable.

He looked up and saw the finishing line just ahead — at last.

While Mac tipped back a bottle of water and poured some of it over his face, Anna was wrapped in a foil blanket and helped towards an ambulance.

She hadn't even had time to thank him.

His cousin was approaching him, face like thunder and Anna smiled to herself. The hare and the tortoise. But Mac was no slow and steady tortoise. She had the feeling that if it hadn't been for her, he would have easily finished miles ahead of his cousin.

'When did you pass me?' he demanded. 'I didn't see you.'

'I hope you have your wallet with you, Martin,' Mac replied calmly. 'If you don't have the cash, I'll accept a cheque. Just make it payable to my chosen charity — the full name of it is on my back.'

'You're not seriously donating it to charity,' Martin spluttered. 'What a waste! It's a grand you wouldn't have had, Mac — at least enjoy it.'

Mac stared at him and Anna realised the concept of enjoying his winnings had never registered. A man to whom money meant nothing?

'Miss . . . ' The paramedic gave her arm a tug. 'This way.'

'I don't need an ambulance,' she said. 'This is such a terrible waste of resources. I'm sure someone could just give me a lift to the hospital.'

She was still protesting in the ambulance. And she'd lost sight of Mac and she had so wanted to thank him properly.

'Are you always as argumentative as this?' the paramedic asked.

'No, it's just I don't like to see waste. I can't bear it, in fact. What if someone else running the marathon has a heart attack and needs urgent medical attention?'

'Will it make you feel better if I tell you another ambulance is on its way to replace us?' The paramedic sighed. 'And we'll head back there after we've dropped you off at the General?'

'What about the St John's people?' she said. 'I'm sure they . . . '

'Have their hands full,' he said. 'Please, just relax and accept that you're going to be taken to hospital.'

She smiled up at him. The reason she was feeling so crabby was that she had been whisked away from Mac so quickly. And not only that, when Fiona

13

turned up with little Cameron, they wouldn't be able to find her and they might worry to hear she'd been carted off in an ambulance.

Cameron was too young to worry, but he was a sensitive child and he'd know something was wrong. And if Fiona brought him to the hospital . . .

She felt tears hot in her eyes. She didn't want him anywhere near a hospital again.

'Come on, now, it's only a swollen foot,' the paramedic said. 'Not the end of the world. You'll run again another day.'

'It's not that,' she bawled as emotion suddenly and embarrassingly over-whelmed her. 'I don't want Cameron to see me in hospital.'

She began to sob, furious with herself for giving way, but unable to do any-thing about it. She'd held on for so long, kept that smile going at all times and in the end she had convinced her-self that she wasn't going to cry — ever.

And she felt so tired. Exhausted, in

fact. And in pain. Worried, too. Her throat ached from the tears. She leaned back and closed her eyes and felt the insistent tears still sliding from her eyes soaking into the pillow under her head as the ambulance headed towards the hospital.

2

'Where'd she go?' Mac asked one of the stewards. 'The girl with the injured foot. She was here just a minute ago.'

'Excuse me,' a pretty young woman with untidy brown hair interrupted. 'I'm looking for someone . . . '

She had a toddler with her, a little boy on reins. Charming child, Mac thought. Cherubic face, dazzling smile and blonde curls.

If things had turned out differently between him and Abigail, who knows, he could have a little boy like that by now. Several of them. But he'd been the one to baulk at the idea of starting a family, further evidence of his selfishness according to Abigail.

'Do you mind?' the steward said.

'No, go ahead, deal with this lady.' Mac smiled. He was in no rush.

'I'm looking for Anna Curtis. She

should be here by now.'

'Anna?' Mac said. 'I'm looking for her, too.'

'How do you know her?' The woman eyed him suspiciously.

'We crossed the finish line together,' he explained. 'She'd hurt her foot. The last I saw she was being taken to see the paramedics. I thought they might have strapped her ankle and she'd be sitting somewhere resting it.'

'Anna? Sitting and resting?' The woman broke into a grin and laughed out loud. 'You don't know her very well at all, do you?'

'Unfortunately I don't know her at all,' Mac said regretfully.

'They took her to hospital,' the steward said, consulting his clipboard. 'Suspected fracture.'

'Oh, goodness,' the woman groaned. 'Trust her.'

'Fracture?' Mac said. 'If I'd known . . .'

'Can you give me directions?' she said sounding panicked. 'I'm not from around here.'

'You've got a car?' Mac asked easily. 'If you'll let me come with you, I can show you the way.'

'You're all right with him, love,' the steward said when she hesitated. 'That's our Dr McKenna. I know his dad.' He added the last with a wink.

'And you are?' Mac asked.

'Fiona. I'm Anna's friend. And this is Cameron. I was looking after him for her. Was she badly hurt?'

'I don't think so,' Mac replied as they made their way to the temporary car park. So this beautiful child was Anna's? Now he came to think of it, there was a resemblance in the shape of their faces — heart-shaped. And the smile of course, the boy had a beautiful smile and so did Anna.

'You don't think so?' Fiona said. 'I thought he said you were a doctor.'

'Well, I didn't take her shoe off and examine the foot,' he said in his defence, though he felt it was a pretty lame excuse. 'She really didn't seem that badly hurt.'

'That's Anna all over,' Fiona said as

she strapped Cameron into his car-seat. 'She never makes a fuss about anything. Don't blame yourself.'

She handed Cameron a book and he opened it and began to study the pictures. *Too cute for words*, Mac thought to himself.

'You say you're not from round here,' Mac said as they were directed out of the car park. 'Turn left at the end of the road and then take an immediate right. Where are you from?'

'Me? Or are you asking about Anna?' she smiled.

'Where is she from?' He grinned. 'I can't understand why we haven't met before.'

'Oh, you don't know the half of it,' Fiona said. 'She is such a fighter. Not for herself you understand, but for others. She fought for her sister and she'll fight for this one in the back. Her whole life has been a struggle, but just now she's getting back on track, settling down.'

'You still haven't answered my question.'

'Bircham Parva,' she said. 'It's a village just over there somewhere. I'm not sure of the geography of the place. I'm from the Midlands myself. We met at university. We were in halls together and have been friends since.'

'I live in White Bircham,' he said. 'Next village along.'

'Fancy that,' Fiona said. 'You're practically neighbours.'

'So, has she lived in the area long? Like I say, I've never seen her about.'

'She brought her sister here to die,' Fiona lowered her voice. 'When there was no hope left, nothing more to be done, Anna brought her here. She could have gone into a hospice, but . . . ' she broke off and bit her lip. 'I've said too much already. It isn't up to me to be telling you any of this. If Anna wants you to know, she'll tell you herself.'

'Take a right just ahead at the roundabout,' Mac said, wondering why he hadn't known about Christa. They must have registered with one of the large practices in town rather than one of the smaller country practices.

'The hospital is on your left. You can see it from here.'

His stomach churned. He was going to see her again. He hadn't lost her. He felt more pleased about that than about completing the marathon and beating his cousin.

When it came to buying a ticket, he had no change on him. Fiona plonked Cameron in his arms.

'Just hang on to him for a second,' she said briskly. 'I'm bound to have some change here somewhere.'

'Hey, there,' he said as Cameron took a good look at his face.

The little boy poked the end of Mac's nose.

'No,' he announced, then his face broke into a beautiful beaming smile that Mac had already seen on Anna's face.

And then it hit him like a sledgehammer. Anna's smile maybe, but whose eyes? Who was his father? Was he around?

21

'There we go,' Fiona's voice interrupted his thoughts. 'We've got two hours. I hope that will be enough. Shall I take him back now?'

'He's all right.' Mac grinned. 'I'll take him.'

'Thanks,' Fiona said. 'He's no lightweight when you've been holding him for a while, believe me.'

But the only thing feeling heavy was Mac's heart.

★　★　★

Duncan Wells held up the x-ray.

'It's a stress fracture, what we call a march fracture because it's a common injury in soldiers,' he said. 'You can't always see the break, but in this case you can see the break here . . . '

'I know what it is,' Anna grumbled. No wonder it hurt. 'What I want to know is how bad it is?'

'It'll be painful for a while . . . '

'Tell me about it.'

'The fracture isn't complete, but if

22

you don't rest it, you could make it so. Keep off it, keep the foot elevated and I'll prescribe some diclofenac.'

'No, thanks,' she said and watched as his jaw dropped. 'I prefer not to have to rely on medication unless it's absolutely necessary.'

'The health service is here for everyone,' he said. 'You included.'

'Hey.' She smiled. 'Nothing personal. It's just the way I am. I don't know how I'm supposed to keep off it, though — I'm starting work at the drop-in centre in town next week.'

'Doing what?'

'More or less what you're doing.' She grinned up at him. 'I'm a doctor.'

It wasn't ideal, but the hours fitted in around Cameron and the childminder, Sandra Cummings. She didn't like leaving him with anyone, but she'd met Sandra several times and she was great with Cameron.

The curtains flew apart and a small figure ran in, little face alight with mischief and expectation and then utter delight when he saw Anna.

He stopped dead in his tracks and held up his arms.

'Up, up, up,' he demanded and as she reached over to lift him, large hands appeared round his middle and lifted him onto the bed beside her.

'There you go,' Mac said. 'There's the lady you've been looking for.'

'Man'na,' he said, peering into her face. But, oh, she was so pleased to see Cameron. Just the sight of him made everything okay.

'Hello, my darling.' She kissed his face. 'I'm so pleased to see you.'

'Oh, Anna,' Fiona said. 'What have you done to yourself, now?'

'Broke my foot.' Anna sighed. 'Just what I need when I'm starting work next week.'

'Doing what?' Mac asked.

'She's a doctor,' Duncan put in, his disapproval of what she planned to do blatantly obvious. 'Working at that drop-in centre in town. It's no place for someone with a broken foot — have you seen how busy they get? It's all rushing around and they're on the go all day. Then there are the stairs.'

Mac couldn't hide his surprise.

'You're a doctor? Why didn't you say?'

'Didn't come up in the conversation.' She smiled. No point wishing she wasn't sat in a soggy T-shirt with her hair all sweaty and stuck to her face.

Not that it mattered what he thought of her. Men didn't figure in her plans.

'If you were looking for work, why didn't you apply for the position in my practice? You must have seen it when you were looking. And I'm based in White Bircham so you could almost walk to work.'

She shrugged.

'You want someone who can cover nights and weekends. Even before I broke my foot I wouldn't have been able to make that kind of commitment. In case you hadn't noticed, there isn't just me to take into consideration.' She looked at Cameron's head and kissed his curls then tightened her hold around him. 'I have to think about this little guy.'

'Blue,' Cameron said, pressing his lips together purposefully and pointing to the doctor's top. 'Blue.'

'That's right, it *is* blue,' Anna cried, her voice trembling with pride, all else forgotten. 'Clever boy. Did you hear that? He's only fifteen months old — how about that?'

He beamed, jabbed the end of her nose with his finger and said, 'No.'

'Nose,' she said.

'No,' he agreed.

'Clever boy.' She smiled, her face, although she didn't realise it, suffused with love so tender that it made her appear to glow.

'Come and work with me, Anna,' Mac said. He didn't know how much experience she had or if she'd get along with the rest of the staff at the Grange Road Practice and frankly he didn't care. He liked her forthright manner and her heart-stopping vulnerability.

'Forget the drop-in centre. You can have a chair in your room to put your foot on to keep it elevated and we can arrange your hours around your child-minder.'

And then there was his father. Patrick McKenna might be semi-retired, but he still took a keen interest in the practice and its staff. He always insisted on a final say in anyone they took on. He'd be furious that Mac had invited this woman to join them without prior consultation.

Everything about this was crazy. Mac only knew that he must not, could not, let Anna go. She hadn't mentioned a Mr Curtis at all, but as there was no one to look after the child at night, he assumed she lived alone. Suddenly his heart no longer felt heavy.

She frowned. A little line puckered in the centre of her brow and her nose wrinkled slightly. Why did he find every single thing about her so attractive and endearing? Even that swollen little foot poking out from under the sheet looked

27

pretty and neat.

He straightened up and gave himself a mental shake. A very hard mental shake. It was one thing to find himself strongly attracted to someone, but to then invite that someone to join his practice and work with him every day was another matter.

He just knew though that the patients would love her down-to-earth manner and the warmth of her ready smile.

'Come for an interview you mean?' she said.

'Yes, obviously.' He grinned, saved.

'I'll have to square it with the drop-in centre,' she mused, but she was clearly giving his proposal serious consideration. 'I mean, it would be letting them down and they might not be able to get a replacement at such short notice. But, then again, given my injury they may be glad not to have me.'

'What?' Fiona said looking horrified. 'Are you mad? It's all arranged, Anna. It took you ages to find that job and even then you said it wasn't perfect and now you're giving it up to work for . . . ' she turned to look at Mac and smiled crookedly. 'The first dishy doctor that comes along and offers you work?'

To his amazement Anna blushed and the dusting of peachy freckles across her nose seemed to glow.

'His dishiness has nothing to do with it,' Anna said levelly. 'His practice is in White Bircham and that just so happens to be the village where my childminder lives. I can't imagine anything more convenient, can you?'

He caught her eye and her blush deepened.

'The surgery is in Grange Road,' he said. 'Call in tomorrow morning at nine and I'll interview you, introduce you to everyone and show you around. Will you be around to drive her?' he asked Fiona.

'I'll be staying on for another day, yes,' Fiona confirmed.

'I'm coming up to the end of my lease on the cottage,' Anna said. 'Do you know of anywhere in White

Bircham that I could rent?'

'I'll ask Mary, our head receptionist. If anyone knows about rentals, she will,' he said. 'I'd best go. I need to get cleaned up for evening surgery at six. It's been great meeting you all. Goodbye, scamp.'

He smiled at Cameron and Cameron reached up his arms. Mac lifted him up and the little boy poked his nose.

'No,' he said.

'Nose,' Mac said, laughing. He loved the way kids found a favourite word and hung on to it until a word came along that they liked better. 'That's right. Be a good boy for your mummy.'

As Mac set Cameron down, he ruffled his hair and smiled warmly at her.

'Just a thought,' he said. 'If you join us, our locum might be able to take over your position at the drop-in centre. I know he was pretty keen on getting that job, but it seems you pipped him to it. It could work out rather well all round.'

But she'd gone rather quiet.

'I'm sorry,' he said. 'I'm assuming rather a lot. Forgive me, Anna, it's just you seem so perfect for us.'

'It isn't that,' Anna said and she twisted her fingers in Cameron's blonde curls making him giggle.

'Christa was his mum,' Fiona enlightened him. 'Cameron is Anna's nephew.'

'I'm sorry,' he said. 'But you look so alike.'

This seemed to please Anna. She smiled up at him.

'Do you really think so? No one has ever said that before.'

'I'm surprised,' he said. 'He's very lucky to have you.'

'No,' she said, kissing the top of the little boy's head. 'I'm the lucky one. He's the best thing that ever happened to me.'

'I really have to go now,' Mac said reluctantly.

'How will you get back?' Fiona asked.

'Oh, I'll find someone to take pity on me and give me a lift back to the

31

village. If all else fails, I'll call someone to come and pick me up.'

'You'll do no such thing,' Anna said, swinging her legs off the bed.

'Can you weight bear, Anna?' Mac said.

'Just about.' She took a step and winced a little and Mac disappeared out of the cubicle, returning moments later with a wheelchair.

'Yes, doctor,' she said. She wasn't going to argue. Mac put Cameron on her lap, then spun the chair, pushing them both into the corridor.

Fiona was trotting along behind, having to run to keep up with his brisk pace. Cameron thought it was hilarious and screamed with laughter as they sped out into the warm sunshine of the car park.

Anna sat down in the car and eased her legs round. Her foot really was dreadfully painful, but it was a pain she knew would ease over the coming days, especially if she took care. Mac waited until she was properly in before closing the door, then he took the handles of the wheelchair and hurried back into the hospital with it.

'Shall I drive off now while I can?' Fiona said. 'We can leave him behind. You never have to see him again.'

'Don't you dare,' Anna said, then she realised Fiona was joking. She kept watching, her eyes on the wing mirror until she saw him striding back towards the car. Her heart gave an unexpected lurch.

'You'll have to give me directions,' Fiona said. 'I've no idea where to go.'

As they drove along, Cameron became drowsy and dropped off to sleep. Mac reclined his seat and smiled tenderly at the flushed, cherubic little face. In the front, Anna was also drowsy. From the back seat he could see her profile, the way her nose turned up a little at the end, her small neat ears and the sooty curve of her eyelashes.

Suddenly he realised Fiona was watching him watching Anna in the rear-view mirror, her eyes crinkling with a smile.

'We'll soon be there,' he said when they'd been driving for a while. 'You can drop me off outside the pub.'

'Which pub?'

'There's only one. You can't miss it. The Green Man.'

Time for a drink before surgery he thought. Just a soft drink, but the company of a few other runners and a bit of harmless banter was just what he needed to make sure that his head was back on straight.

Like Cameron, Anna was asleep when he got out of the car. She looked just as peaceful, just as cherubic as her nephew. Asleep, her face had lost that troubled look.

'Tomorrow at nine,' he whispered to Fiona. 'You'll remind her?'

'Don't worry,' Fiona smiled. 'She'll be there.'

'Thanks for the lift.'

He shut the door quietly and stood outside the pub watching as the car disappeared down the road.

3

Anna stirred when Fiona pulled up outside her rented cottage. She blinked, sat upright and turned, the smile freezing on her lips.

'He's gone,' Fiona said. 'I already dropped him off.'

'Oh.'

'Disappointed?'

'Of course not,' Anna said, though it was a lie and the truth all mingled in together. She sensed something very special about Mac and couldn't deny she was attracted to him, but she could be strong — she knew she could — and she would resist the attraction. But he was gorgeous and he'd come to her rescue and she wasn't naïve enough to think resisting him would be easy. He was good with Cameron, too. Her nephew didn't take to everyone, but he'd certainly taken to Mac.

What was important was to do what was right for Cameron and that was just what she was doing. By going for the job in the village instead of the town, joining a real family practice, she was doing the best she could.

* * *

'So you're telling me that you met this woman during the marathon and offered her a job on the spot?' Patrick McKenna said incredulously. 'You've done some stupid things in your time, Mac, but this has to register way up there between marrying Abigail and smashing your motorbike into a tree!'

'The first was a mistake, the second an accident,' Mac replied. 'Taking on Anna will be neither. She could be just what the practice needs, Dad.'

'Or perhaps she's just what you need,' Patrick mused.

'It's not like that,' Mac said quickly, too quickly.

'Isn't it? Well, I'll reserve judgement

until I've seen her, but if she turns out to be an old dragon with scales and a frown to freeze fire, I'll be surprised.'

'Of course she isn't an old dragon.' Mac laughed. 'She's . . . well, she's good looking I suppose. Petite, blonde, green-eyed . . . ' he broke off.

'Considering you only met her today, you seem to have noticed an awful lot about her.' Patrick's eyes sparkled as he laughed. 'How old is she? No, wait; let me guess — around thirty? And she's single? Unattached? And let me see, you're thirty-five, also unattached . . . Hmm?'

'You're the one who keeps turning people down, Dad,' Mac said, feeling more and more uncomfortable.

'Have you eaten today?'

'I guess not,' he said wearily. It had been a long day and food hadn't figured high on his list of priorities.

'You guess? It's almost ten o'clock. You've run a marathon, spent all evening seeing patients and you haven't thought to stoke up? Even the best engines fail without fuel, Mac. Let me get you some-thing.'

'I'll be all right, Dad,' Mac said. 'I just want to get home and get to bed.'

'Promise you'll eat — and more than a packet of crisps and a few biscuits,' Patrick said. 'And switch over the night service to me. I'll take any calls.'

Back home, Mac opened the cup-board where he kept his supply of junk food, then remembered his promise to his father.

He looked in the fridge and found a ready meal which had gone out of date. He took off the outer packaging and shoved it in the microwave, confident that anything nasty lurking in there would be killed off.

He'd never been much of a cook. Oh, he made the effort if his father joined him for a meal, but saw no point in going to any trouble for himself.

It wasn't the most appetising meal in the world, but it was hot and it filled a hole and when he finally dropped into his bed, exhausted, he slept soundly for seven hours until his alarm woke him.

★ ★ ★

'Do you think it'll be a proper interview?' Anna said nervously. 'Do I look all right? Am I doing the right thing?'

Fiona stopped chewing on her toast and looked up at her friend.

'It's a bit late to be worrying about that, isn't it?' she said. 'As I recall, he offered you the job, you practically bit his hand off when you snatched at it and the deal was sealed. Had they given you something in the hospital to addle your brain?'

'You think I'm making a mistake.' Anna sighed, slumping in the chair.

'I don't know what to think, Anna,' Fiona said. 'He seemed like a really nice guy and on the face of it the job could be a whole lot better than the other one you had lined up. Cam's not always going to be a baby and when he's older

39

you're going to need something more stable. If you're still around here that is.'

'Oh, I'll still be around here,' Anna said determinedly. 'Christa and I chose this place together. She wanted Cameron to grow up somewhere — for want of a better word — nice. Somewhere he'd go to the same school with the same friends and not have to keep moving around. She wanted him to have the stability and roots that we never had.'

Fiona nodded her understanding, then a mischievous smile stole across her face.

'And what about Mac?'

'What about him?'

'Oh, come on, Anna,' Fiona burst out. 'He's gorgeous! Don't tell me you hadn't noticed. He's got that husky voice that turns your insides to treacle and those stunning eyes. Did you see them? Have you ever seen eyes so blue? Everything about the guy is so sexy.'

'Well, I guess he's okay,' Anna said.

She didn't need Fiona to tell her any of that, she was only human after all and wasn't immune to such things. 'But you know me and guys — we don't mix. Never have, never will.'

'Rubbish!' Fiona cried. 'Just because you had a few bad experiences years ago doesn't mean you have to write off the rest of your life.'

'Stop it, Fi,' Anna warned.

'But it's true,' Fiona said sadly. 'Look at you, the way you're cutting yourself off. Mac's a nice guy — you could do a lot worse.'

'And he may not even be interested anyway,' Anna said. 'He was telling me how hard it was to get staff for his practice. Maybe he's just desperate.'

Anna helped Cameron to spoon his cereal into his mouth. He was at an age where he wanted to feed himself, but hadn't quite got his hand-to-mouth coordination right. He squealed and wrenched his hand away from her and plunged his spoon into his bowl.

'Let me help you, Cameron,' she said

softly. He allowed her to help him guide the spoon to his mouth and he smiled as the cereal went in. Then he flicked the spoon out of his mouth and showered Anna with milk and bits of cereal.

'Why don't you give him toast?' Fiona said as Anna wiped the milk off her face and shirt. 'It would probably be a lot less messy.'

'Because he likes cereal,' Anna replied.

'No more,' Cameron said and pushed his bowl away so determinedly it caught on the lip of his high chair tray and before Anna could stop it, had gone over the edge and splattered her skirt.

Fiona giggled. Anna couldn't help laughing, too, as she dabbed at the milk with kitchen paper. She knew it was wrong to laugh and might encourage him to do it on purpose next time, but sometimes she felt that if she didn't laugh, she might cry.

There wasn't time to change her clothes as well as Cameron's, so Anna mopped up the milk as best she could and decided she'd just have to do.

She was wearing wide, sensible, supportive shoes. They were flat and unflattering, but they took some of the pressure off her foot and she knew it was just a matter of time before the pain began to ease.

She was just grateful that Fiona was here today to drive her over to White Bircham even if she did have a tendency to try and run Anna's life. And she was doing the right thing. Working in the village would be so much better than having to drive all the way to town every day. She'd get to know her patients here and would see more of Cameron. And who knows, she might even find somewhere suitable to rent in the village and be closer to work.

'It could all work out rather well, couldn't it?' she said out loud.

'Well, it won't if we don't get going,' Fiona replied, handing Anna her bag.

White Bircham was a larger village

than Bircham Parva and even prettier with a picturesque Norman church overlooking the green. Anna knew it a little from her visits to Sandra who lived in a large square house opposite the church from where she ran her childminding business.

The village nestled at the end of a long leafy road where trees bowed over making an archway and you felt as if you were entering somewhere rather special and almost magical. There was just the one way in or out of the village unlike in Bircham Parva which was on a busy main road. This would be a much safer place for Cameron to be and that thought reinforced that she was doing this for him, not herself.

Some men were working on the trees that bordered the road. They were tree surgeons, strapped into harnesses and hanging from some of the sturdier branches as they worked with their chainsaws to trim the trees.

They passed the little village school, a traditional old building. Anna could see

Cameron going there when he was old enough, she really could. She could see herself walking to the village shop and taking picnics to the forest.

Anna felt a strange quiver of fear in her stomach. Was she really doing the right thing for the right reasons?

Grange Road ran up a hill where trees and shrubs grew in abundance in large front gardens with long, sweeping driveways.

'Very posh,' Fiona murmured.

The surgery was easy to spot with a large sign outside and the whole of the front garden turned into a car park, but shrubs still bordered the edges and hanging baskets bloomed at the front of the big, old house.

Further up the hill, Anna could see what must be the Grange from which the road took its name, a large impressive building peeking out between a border of massive old trees with a red roof and leaded windows that reflected the sunshine.

'Wish me luck,' Anna said. She was

feeling more nervous about this than she'd ever felt about an interview in her life.

'Knock 'em dead! Remember you're a good doctor. You might be here because the dishy doctor likes the look of you, but you've got credentials.'

★　★　★

Mac glanced out of the window and saw Anna getting out of Fiona's car. Off went his heart again, hammering away like a pneumatic drill behind his ribs. Apart from the limp she looked great. Her hair was tied back without the wisps that had escaped during the run yesterday framing her face.

'She's here,' he said, recapturing his breath and turning to his father who had come in specially to meet her. 'Everybody ready?'

He looked around the room at all the trusted individuals who made the Grange Road Practice what it was, friendly and caring for the community.

There was Mary Steele, the head receptionist; Pam Flowers, the head practice nurse; and Mac's cousin, Martin McKenna, their practice manager.

He left the room and met Anna as she came in the door. Her face lit up when she saw him. Relief? Or pleasure? She looked stunning.

'How's the foot?' he asked.

'Sore,' she said. 'Have you had second thoughts, because . . . '

'No second thoughts,' he interrupted with a smile. 'You?'

'None as yet.'

'Good,' his smile widened.

She looked up at him with those pretty green eyes and he offered his arm which she took with a grateful smile.

'I'll organise some crutches for you,' he said.

He stopped outside the room.

'You ready for this?' he asked.

'As ready as I'll ever be.'

'Good.' He smiled and opened the door. 'Everyone, this is Doctor Anna

Curtis who I hope will be joining us on a permanent basis. Anna, this is my father, Patrick McKenna.'

She shook Patrick's hand and Mac could see his father was already impressed. It was that smile of hers.

'Martin McKenna, my cousin — you saw him briefly yesterday as we overtook him at the marathon. He's our practice manager.'

Martin took her hand and held on to it far too long.

'A pleasure to meet you,' Martin drawled.

'Pleased to meet you, Anna. I'm Pam Flowers, practice nurse.'

And no sooner had she finished shaking Pam's hand than Mary stepped forward and being Mary she dispensed with formalities and simply gave Anna a hug which seemed to throw Anna off balance for a moment. She hesitated for a few seconds, then hugged Mary back. Her hesitation hinted at someone who wasn't used to giving or receiving affection.

'It's lovely to meet you. Mac's told us a lot about you and we all think you sound ideal, but I expect you want to see if we pass muster.'

Mac couldn't have been more pleased with the warm welcome they were offering. It confirmed what he already knew, that he wasn't wrong in his judgement and that she would fit in here perfectly well.

Martin was the only fly in the ointment, but Martin was a law unto himself. They all sat down and Mac presented Anna with a chair on which to rest her foot. He feared she might feel awkward, but the others spoke to her as if she were already a member of the team, already a friend.

'I've brought some references along,' she said and as she got them out of her case, Martin snatched them from her hands.

Mac rose to his feet and was steadied by his father's hand on his arm.

The jumped-up little . . . Mac was furious.

'May I hang on to these?' Martin said. 'I need to check they're in order.'

'Of course,' Anna said, not in the least fazed.

Mac sank slowly back to his seat.

'You can take them and do that now, Martin,' Patrick said, effectively dismissing him from the room. 'Off you go.' When he'd gone, Patrick continued. 'Has anyone any further questions for Anna?'

'I don't have a question exactly,' Mary said. 'Mac said that you were looking for a place to rent in White Bircham. Is that right?'

'Yes,' Anna sat up straighter. 'You know of somewhere?'

'I think I do,' Mary said and bit her lip. She was a dear lady and Mac was incredibly fond of her. 'Until quite recently my mother lived with me in an annexe I had built on my cottage. It's cosy, easy to maintain, small and neat with a good sized bedroom with French doors opening onto the garden.'

Mary's eyes misted slightly.

'It sounds lovely, Mary, and I thank you from the bottom of my heart,' Anna said. 'But I really need somewhere a little bigger. My nephew, Cameron, lives with me and although we could share a room at a pinch, he'll soon be at an age when he needs his own space.'

Mary's eyes cleared and she smiled broadly.

'I know that,' she said. 'Perhaps I didn't make myself clear, dear. My cottage is quite large and in all honesty when I get home from work the last thing I feel like doing is housework. I've been thinking about moving into the annexe, but I would be worried about letting the house to strangers. And you're not a stranger are you, dear? You'll be one of us.' Her dark eyes twinkled as she leaned forward and placed her hand on Anna's knee.

'And I'll be on hand for babysitting if ever you need me and for keeping an eye on Cameron when you cover nights.'

'In that case, I could cover night

calls,' Anne said thoughtfully. 'Cameron always sleeps through, so he wouldn't be any trouble.'

Mac shot a look at his father, a look that said, 'I told you so.' She was already thinking like one of them and she was so right it was almost painful.

4

Anna sat back in the chair and let out her breath in a rush. She felt very suspicious about all this. She couldn't help herself. All her life she'd struggled and she'd had more knock backs than she could remember, but here she was being offered the perfect job in the perfect village and she even had a woman who seemed to be offering herself as a mother figure.

She just couldn't take it all in. She was overwhelmed by the kindness and warmth of these people. If only she'd known about this practice when she moved to Bircham Parva with Christa, she would have registered with them instead of the busy practice in town. And if she had, in the care of these people, would Christa's last weeks have been any more bearable?

'I ... I ... ' she began and

something happened to her that had never happened to her in her life before. She found herself struggling to find words to express her gratitude, her throat was tightening and she felt alarmingly close to tears for the second time in two days. Could she possibly find it anywhere inside herself to trust these people with her and Cameron's future when she had never in her life trusted anyone but herself?

'Anna?' Mac said. 'What do you think? Will we do?'

'Yes.' She laughed and bit back tears. Would they do? She felt as if she'd stepped into a dream.

Then the door opened and Martin walked in, a grim look on his face.

'Before you make any rash decisions,' he said coldly. 'I think you'd better take a look at this. Doctor Curtis here doesn't exactly have an unblemished record.'

Martin handed the paper to Patrick who looked it over, raised his eyebrows slightly and passed it on to Mac.

'What of it?' Mac asked. 'This was in

the past. Doctor Curtis was exonerated of any blame. I don't see it as being of any relevance.'

Anna's breath caught in her throat. She felt almost relieved. Up until now things had been going far too smoothly.

'Her sister is a drug addict,' Martin said, driving his point home by tapping his finger on the desk. 'She stole from the pharmacy where Doctor Curtis was in general practice. What if she turns up here looking for a quick fix? What if she brings her friends? And why has there been such a long period of unemployment?'

'That's enough, Martin!' Mac blazed, jumping to his feet.

'I'm sorry . . . ' she began.

'You have nothing to apologise for, Anna,' Mac said, still glowering at his cousin. 'I think Martin should apologise to you for speaking out of turn when he doesn't have the full facts.'

Anna lifted her hand.

'No apology necessary,' she said coolly and turned to address Martin. 'My sister is dead, Mr McKenna. And it's on the record that when I found out that she was involved in the break in at the pharmacy, I reported her to the police myself. Perhaps if you'd read on you would have discovered that for yourself. It's not something I feel I have to hide, nor do I feel I have to defend my sister to you or anyone else. You know nothing of her life and the hardships she faced. As for my period of unemployment, I stopped work to nurse my sister when she was dying.'

The colour drained from Martin's face leaving a pair of red spots on his cheeks. Mac seemed satisfied that Anna was perfectly capable of fighting her own battles and sat down again.

'Yes, well,' Martin blustered. 'I just wanted to make sure everyone was aware of it, that's all.'

'Highly commendable of you,' Anna said, smiling tightly. 'Perhaps I should also tell you that my nephew threw his breakfast cereal at me this morning hence the stains on my skirt, but he's only fifteen months old and I don't think you need concern yourself about his possible delinquency and descent into a life of crime just yet, do you?'

Patrick's expression was grave, but she saw a smile skirting around Mac's mouth and knew he was having trouble keeping a neutral expression on his face.

'Are we all agreed?' Mac asked.

There was a murmur of agreement and he looked up at Martin who was still on his feet, still scowling.

'Martin?'

'Yes, whatever,' Martin said sulkily. 'It seems you've already made up your minds anyway.'

'Anna? Will you join us?'

'I'd love to,' she said. 'Thank you so much.'

'That's great,' Mac shook her hand firmly. 'Mary will show you around, but I've got patients waiting. Will a week be long enough for you to sort out your affairs and move here?'

'A week will be great.' Anna laughed.

★ ★ ★

'Mac's wife left him,' Mary said when she finished the tour of the surgery with a visit to the room that would be Anna's. 'Abigail was never cut out to be a doctor's wife. She resented every minute he spent with his patients instead of being grateful that she was married to a decent, caring man.'

'You don't really have to tell me any of this,' Anna said gently.

'I'm telling you because if I don't, someone else will, and I want you to hear the real story.'

'Martin, you mean?'

Mary scowled.

'He's a mischief maker as you've probably already gathered. He went to medical school, but didn't see it out, whereas Mac,' her face softened into an expression of almost motherly affection. 'Oh, don't get me wrong, he's had his wild moments, but he's a hard worker. It'll be lovely to have you in the cottage. I know you'll love it and I can't wait to meet little Cameron.'

Anna stepped outside into the sunshine using the crutches Mac had found for her just as Fiona was turning into the car park pushing the buggy.

'Man'na!' Cameron squealed, kicking his feet against his chair.

Fiona bent down, unfastened his harness and he slithered to the floor, landed on his feet and ran towards Anna, his arms already reaching for her. Her heart lifted as it did every time she looked at him and she scooped him up in her arms and held him high, letting her crutches fall to the ground. Fiona picked up the crutches, took Cameron back and handed them to her.

'We've been all round the village — twice. Cam particularly liked the ducks around the pond and the tractor we saw in a field. You were in there ages. I take it things went well?'

'I've not only got a job, I've also got somewhere to live,' Anna said, so pleased that she could hardly contain herself.

'Congratulations.' Fiona grinned. 'And the village pub is gorgeous. Shall we head over there for an early lunch?'

Some time later, it was a very mellow Anna who sat in the front of Fiona's car as they headed out of White Bircham down the leafy road.

'Oh, no,' Fiona said as she slowed to a crawl. 'What's happened here?'

Anna opened her eyes. Cameron was asleep in the back.

'What is it?' she asked sleepily.

'I don't know . . . These tree guys. I think they want us to stop . . . '

Anna pulled herself upright, alarm bells clanging in her head.

'You're right! Pull in, Fiona. There's been an accident.'

A man in a hard yellow hat was running towards them. Up in the trees the ropes still dangled as if they'd been left behind in a hurry.

Anna guessed what had happened when she saw the dangling ropes, and her heart sank.

He leaned in Fiona's open window,

his ruddy face crumpled with fear.

'Have you got a mobile phone? None of us can get a signal.'

'What's happened?' Anna leaned across and asked.

'One of my men is hurt — he accidently cut his ropes with his chainsaw . . .'

He'd barely uttered the words when Anna flung her door open.

'No, love,' the man said urgently. 'We just need a phone, that's all. Best you stay in your car.'

She ignored him and grabbed her crutches.

'Don't go over there,' the man said, hurrying along beside Anna. 'There's a lot of blood — he's hurt pretty bad. You don't want to . . .'

'I'm a doctor,' Anna cut in. 'I may be able to help.'

He looked taken aback, then pleased.

'Well, thank goodness for small mercies,' he said. 'I'm Colin Harker.'

'Anna Curtis,' Anna said.

Behind them, Fiona spun the car round.

'I can't get a signal,' she shouted

through her open window. 'I'll drive back to the surgery and get help.'

'Drive carefully, Fi,' Anna called. 'Don't forget Cam's in the back.'

She wondered briefly why none of the men had thought to drive into the village for help, then realised the only vehicles they had were tractors

'Have you moved him?' she asked, seeing the guy lying on his back.

'He's as he fell,' Colin said. 'We don't dare move him.'

'What's his name?'

'Gavin,' Colin said raggedly and his voice broke as he continued. 'Gavin Harker. He's my son. My oldest boy.'

Anna handed her crutches to one of the men and knelt down beside the injured man.

'Gavin, can you hear me? My name's Anna. I'm a doctor and I'm going to try and make you more comfortable until help arrives.'

He mumbled something incoherent.

'Can you tell me where you hurt most, Gavin?'

'Chest,' he gasped. 'Leg.'

He moved his hand to touch his chest and winced with pain.

'Are you having trouble breathing, Gavin?'

'Yes,' he whispered. 'Feels . . . odd.'

'It would.' She nodded. 'Anyone have a knife?'

'What do you want a knife for?'

'I want to get his shirt off — I need to cut it away. And I'm going to have to cut away his trousers. There's not much I can do, but I can get him ready for when the ambulance arrives.'

She was handed a knife with a sharp, curved blade and she used it to cut his clothing away. Judging by the movement of his chest, she was sure his lung had collapsed. The left side wasn't moving at all.

'Does your neck hurt at all, Gavin?'

'Everything hurts.'

'I know it's difficult, but please try to keep as still as you can.'

'Isn't there anything you can do?' Colin Harker asked, desperation giving his voice an edge. He was suffering in the way only a parent can and Anna knew he'd be wishing it was him lying there rather than his son. She knew how painful it was to watch someone you loved suffering.

'Try not to worry. Help will soon be here.'

She prayed she was right. She turned her attention to his leg. The break was a bad one and the shattered bones had pierced the skin. The wound was bleeding heavily.

'How long has it been?' she asked. 'Since my friend went for help?'

'Ten minutes?' Colin said. He was on his knees beside Anna, unshed tears turning the whites of his eyes pink. 'Is he going to be all right?'

'He will be if we can get him to hospital quickly,' Anna said and reached out to squeeze the terrified man's arm. 'And we will, Colin.'

'Thank you,' he whispered, battling tears.

'I haven't done anything,' Anna said,

feeling helpless, and at that point, a blue car came tearing down the road and skidded to a halt behind the tractors. In the distance she could hear sirens.

'It's Mac!' Colin shouted.

Mac jumped from his car, grabbed his bag and ran over. Anna quickly got to her feet, happy to see him, even happier to see his medical bag.

'Please tell me that ambulance I can hear is headed our way,' she said.

'It is.' He smiled tightly, his eyes raking Gavin from head to toe, taking in the scene. 'Have you been able to do anything for him, Anna? Fiona was in a bit of a state. She said something about an accident with a chainsaw.'

Anna quickly told him what had happened. While he listened he unconsciously reached out, his fingers circling her arm as he stooped slightly to hear what she was saying.

'Not as bad as I feared then,' Mac said when she'd finished. 'I thought I was going to find amputated limbs.

Don't worry about Fiona and Cameron, Anna. Mary is taking care of them.'

He listened to Gavin's chest.

'No breath sounds this side. You're right, Anna. His lung has collapsed.' He looked at Anna. 'Let's get a cannula in. By the time we've done that, the ambulance should be here.'

He was right. The sirens were getting louder, coming closer through the narrow country lanes.

'Is he going to be all right, Mac?' Colin asked.

'Of course he is,' Mac replied. 'But how the hell did this happen, Colin? You don't run a careless team and Gavin of all people . . . '

'I have no idea. He knows the rules, he's not one to mess about,' Colin said despairingly. 'I don't have a clue how this happened, Mac. I wish I did.'

'I think he yelled before he cut through the ropes,' one of the other men said. 'As if he'd been startled.'

Anna saw it then, the slightly swollen, livid, red mark on Gavin's neck.

'Were you stung, Gavin?' she asked.

'There were some hornets up there,' Colin said. 'But they aren't normally aggressive. Gav's never been happy round stinging insects.'

'You're lucky it didn't provoke a full on attack,' Mac said. 'If the hornet that stung Gavin was protecting a nest, it could well have released a scent to warn others.'

They all looked up as if expecting a swarm of angry insects to descend.

The paramedics arrived and set about immobilising Gavin's cervical spine with a collar while Anna helped Mac prepare the chest drain.

Colin's eyes widened when at last air gurgled out of his son's chest.

'What's that noise? Is that coming out of him?'

'It's the air coming out of Gavin's chest. His lung will reinflate now,' Anna explained. 'The pain will ease and his breathing will become easier.'

'Will you go in the ambulance with him, Anna?' Mac murmured as the paramedics moved Gavin onto the ambulance. 'I'll follow in my car with Colin. You're okay with that?'

She looked into those intense blue eyes and had the thought that she would be okay with anything he'd like to suggest. She shook herself.

'Yes, that's fine.'

* * *

'Wait here, Colin,' Mac said when they reached the reception

Colin sank onto a chair. He was white faced and trembling. The poor guy. Bad enough seeing anyone hurt like that, but his own son? It must have been a terrible few seconds when Gavin fell from the tree. They worked at such great heights and usually with such enormous care, accidents like this were thankfully rare. As Mac walked through to resus, Anna met him.

'How's Colin?' she asked.

'Terrified,' he said. 'Gavin?'

'It's pretty bad, Mac — his ribs are a

mess, but there's no indication of spinal damage.' She went on to fill him in on all the details.

'I don't want to leave Colin alone,' Mac said. 'He's pretty shaken up.'

'Okay, I'll bring you both some tea when I come back.'

'Excellent.' Mac grinned. 'I've called Mary. She's going to take Fiona and Cameron back to her cottage until you get back.'

'Thank you.'

★ ★ ★

'It doesn't look as if he has any spinal injury, Colin, but he's still having problems breathing, so for now they've put him on a ventilator.'

'What?' Colin sat upright, the fear apparent in his eyes. 'Is he awake?'

'No, they'll have put him out for that. He won't feel a thing — he's out of it now for a while. The machine will breathe for him and he'll be a lot more comfortable. He was in a lot of pain, sleep's the best thing for him.'

He became aware of someone standing in front of him and looked down at a pair of mucky, sturdy shoes. When he looked up it was to see Anna standing there with a cup in each hand as promised.

'Tea,' she said, handing them each a cup then sitting beside Colin.

'He will get better, Colin. He's young and strong and given the extent of his rib fractures he's actually doing rather well.'

Colin took a sip from his cup.

'Oh, heck,' he muttered. 'What am I going to tell the wife? She'll kill me.' Then he looked at Anna. 'Didn't you have crutches?'

'I did,' she said, biting her lip. 'But I left them at the scene. Sorry, Mac.'

5

When Colin's wife Hannah arrived, Mac and Anna slipped away. She seemed to be coping better than Colin, but then she hadn't seen her son's broken and battered body on the ground.

When Mac pulled up outside Mary's cottage, Anna was asleep. He touched her arm gently after gazing at her for a few seconds.

'Anna, we're here,' he said softly and her eyes flashed open, her sleepy smile a joy to see.

'Already,' she stretched and he looked away.

'That's Mary's cottage just there.'

'Wow,' she breathed.

'Yes,' he said, seeing it as if for the first time through her eyes. It was a beautiful cottage. Palest pink painted walls, thatched roof, roses round the door and an abundance of flowers growing in the front garden.

'It's beautiful,' she said, gazing at it as she pushed open the car door.

'They'll be in the garden. Come this way.'

She followed him down the side of the cottage, under a wooden pergola dripping with honeysuckle and into a colourful cottage garden.

Cameron was squatting down playing with a bucket and spade while Mary sat on a swing hammock watching him.

'Cameron,' Anna said, and at the sound of her voice, he looked up and fell backwards onto his bottom. But he was fast to his feet and running towards her in his lop-sided, unsteady way, calling her name.

'Someone's pleased to see you,' Mac remarked, swallowing back the lump in his throat as Anna bent down and scooped the child up in her arms.

Mac had only vague memories of his own mother. Most of his memories were gained from studying photographs, but one thing he could remember was her voice. Soft and musical. She'd been almost ten years older than his father and she had been forty when Mac was born. When he was two years old, she was diagnosed with a motor neurone disease. By the time he was five years old, she was dead. There was no warm and loving aunt to step in and take her place, just his father who had been the same age as Mac was now when he found himself widowed with a young son.

Thank goodness for Mary. She'd collected him from school, sewn his name tags into his uniforms and created wild and wonderful costumes for school pageants.

'Fiona had to go, dear,' Mary said. 'She didn't want to, but she said something about having to get back to the Midlands tonight. I said it would be all right. I can run you home . . . '

'No need,' Mac put in. 'I'll see Anna and Cameron get home this evening, Mary. Thank you.'

Anna sat on the grass with Cameron while Mary went off to get the cup of tea she insisted Anna should have.

'I have to go,' Mac said. 'I'm going to have a waiting room full of irate patients and if they find out I've been over here drinking tea with Mary, they'll probably lynch me.'

'I doubt that.' Anna grinned up at him. 'When Mary gave me the tour, I heard patients in the waiting room talking about you. They weren't after lynching you, believe me.'

He looked embarrassed.

'Well.' He glanced at his watch. 'I shouldn't be too long. I only have a handful of patients to see. Do you mind waiting here?'

'Look, Mac, I can always get a taxi,' she began.

'No,' he said quickly. 'Don't do that. Wait for me — please, Anna.'

'Okay, Mac, thank you.'

Cameron got to his feet and waved as Anna watched the one guy in the world who had any chance of changing her mind about men walk away.

'Here we are,' Mary trilled as she came out into the garden.

'I hope he hasn't been a bother.'

'Oh, bless you, dear, of course he hasn't been a bother. He's been a pleasure to have around. He's very bright for his age, isn't he?'

'Yes,' Anna agreed proudly. 'My sister was, too.'

'Are you all right, dear?' Mary's kindly eyes were staring at her.

'It's been a rather long day,' Anna replied with a smile.

'You can tell me about Gavin and everything that happened when you've had your tea. Then we can sort out proper arrangements for you to move in. And while you relax I'll tell you about some of the people in the village and surrounding area. The practice covers several villages . . . ' Her voice carried on and Anna listened at some level, but her mind had gone rather blank.

It was soon way past Cameron's

bedtime and Anna was going to absolutely insist on calling a taxi when she heard a car pull up at the front and then moments later the slam of a door.

'Sorry,' Mac said as he walked into the garden. 'I didn't mean to take so long, but . . . you know how it is.'

Yes, Anna thought. *I do know how it is. You won't rush your patients through their allotted time and you end up running late and surgery runs over.* It was for this reason that Anna wanted to join this practice so badly.

'It's no problem, Mac.' Anna smiled. 'It's been lovely sitting out here with Mary. She's been telling me all about the village — and everyone in it.'

'Whatever she said about me — don't believe a word of it!' Mac laughed.

'So you're not a great doctor, loved by all, then?' Anna smiled.

'I'm so looking forward to having you take over the cottage, dear,' Mary said happily. 'I think you were meant for this place.'

Anna thought so, too.

Mac had already fitted the car seat into the back of his car and he strapped Cameron in while Anna got into the front passenger seat.

'I seem to have spent most of the day in your car,' Anna said.

'Is that so terrible?'

She answered with a smile.

They waved goodbye as they drove off and, as always, a few minutes in the car had Cameron nodding off to sleep.

'I don't know about you, but I'm starving,' Mac said. 'What do you prefer, Indian or Chinese?'

'Chinese.'

'Anything you won't eat?'

'No, not really,' she said. 'But really, you don't have to . . . '

'Oh, I do have to,' he interrupted. 'I'm famished and there just happens to be a great Chinese restaurant in Bircham Parva. There's a menu in the glove box. Have a look. See what you fancy. I'll drop you off at home and while you're settling Cameron down, I'll pick up the food.'

'No, really, I . . . '

'Please,' he turned to glance at her, eyes imploring. 'If you won't eat with me, I won't have any excuse not to go straight home and cook my own supper and if you knew how bad a cook I was you would never condemn me to that.'

Put like that, how could she resist?

'Just . . . just plain Singapore noodles,' she said, her mouth beginning to water as she looked at the menu. 'And, um . . . prawn satay.'

He pulled up on the drive. It was a nice little house, but it wasn't a patch on Mary's. In fact, now she'd sampled life in White Bircham, this didn't feel like home any more. As she got out of the car, she hoped Christa would understand why she was moving out of the cottage they'd chosen together.

Yes, she would, she thought resolutely. Christa trusted her to do what was right for Cameron and this was right, she knew it.

Mac watched as Anna gently and expertly lifted the sleeping toddler from his car seat. Anna had already handed him her keys, but he was so engrossed in watching her with the child that he forgot about opening the front door until he realised she was looking up at him expectantly.

'Sorry, I was miles away,' he said with a grin and turned to slip the key in the lock. Thank goodness his hands were steady.

'Thank you,' she said over the top of Cameron's tousled head. 'I should be able to get him into his pyjamas and into bed without waking him up. Hang on to my keys and let yourself in when you get back with the food.'

★   ★   ★

He waited until she was inside before going back to his car. He felt like jumping up in the air and kicking his heels together. *Don't get carried away,* he told himself. *This isn't a date. Just a takeaway meal, nothing to get excited about.* But how could he help himself when she'd looked up at him with those sleepy green eyes and that gentle smile?

There was a queue at the takeaway. He should have called ahead with his order. This was going to take all night! Precious time he could have been spending with Anna was trickling away from him.

★　★　★

Cameron's eyes blinked open just as Anna was fastening his nappy.

'Go back to sleep, sweetie,' she murmured as she lay him in his cot.

Mac was coming back. *Stop smiling. He's just bringing food, that's all. Doesn't mean anything and even if it did, you aren't going to let anything happen, are you?*

Anna yawned and sat down on the floor beside the cot.

'I don't know about you, Cam,' she said sleepily. 'But I'm beat. I'm just going to put my head down for a moment while you go to sleep.'

She piled up some floor cushions and rested her head on them. In a moment she'd go downstairs and put some plates in the oven to warm . . . Maybe open a bottle of wine . . .

* * *

Mac let himself into the cottage to be greeted by silence. He expected soft music — something, anything but the quiet broken only by the loud ticking of the hall clock.

'Anna?' he called softly.

He went through to the sitting room. Lights off. Curtains still open. He turned on a lamp and closed the curtains. The kitchen was also deserted.

He put the food down on the kitchen table and went upstairs, aware of every creaking step on the way. He followed the soft glow of a night light into the small room at the back. Cameron was asleep, arms and legs splayed, cheeks pink, lashes making dark sweeps across his skin. On the floor beside the cot,

81

head back on a pile of cushions, Anna.

The sight of her took his breath away. Was it really possible he'd only met her yesterday?

Cameron's legs were tangled with his sheets. Gently Mac untangled him and covered him up. Then he turned his attention to Anna, hunkering down beside her and reaching out to touch her. His fingers grazed her cheek. She looked so innocent asleep, so untroubled. Gone was that funny little frown line between her brows as if awake she constantly found life a puzzle.

A curl of hair stuck damply to her cheek and he brushed it away and that's when her eyes flipped open and she looked at first scared, then pleased, then annoyed.

'What are you doing?' she demanded, scrambling to sit up.

'Shh,' he pressed his fingers to his lips and looked at the cot.

She hesitated, sniffed the air and her face relaxed as her eyes softened and her mouth curved into a smile.

'You brought food,' she whispered, holding out her hand so he could pull her to her feet. She was still sleepy and bounced unsteadily into his chest. He had to hold her with his free hand to steady her.

'Sorry,' they said in unison, then both laughed and said it again. 'Sorry.'

Downstairs they unpacked the Chinese food. Anna reached into a cupboard for plates.

'Hey.' Mac laughed. 'No plates. The only way to eat Chinese food is straight from the carton. No washing up.'

'Suits me,' she said. 'Wine?'

'Damn. I didn't get any. It was busy in the Chinese and by the time I left I was so glad to get out of there . . . '

She was already opening another cupboard, reaching in for a bottle.

'Shiraz?' she said.

'Sounds good to me.'

She took two large wine glasses down and put them on the table.

When the glasses were full, Mac lifted his.

'To Christa,' he said.

'To Christa,' Anna echoed, but her voice was strained as if her throat was tight. 'I'm sorry for the way I jumped when you woke me. Once, one of Christa's . . . friends,' she almost spat the word, 'broke into our house while we were asleep. I woke to find him going through my things.'

'Your reaction was perfectly understandable,' he said, his voice calm.

'You're not eating,' she said when she realised he was watching her eat.

'I don't think I can do this,' he muttered.

'Sorry?' she looked up. 'You said something.'

'Will he be off for the night?' he asked. 'Cameron?'

'Yes, he should sleep through. He's always been an angel. Even when he was waking for night-time feeds, he used to go straight back to sleep after.'

He loved the way her features softened when she spoke about Cameron. In fact, her whole body seemed softer. Or maybe that was just the wine on an empty stomach after a busy day.

To take his mind off Anna and the inappropriate direction his thoughts were taking, Mac ate his food and drank his wine and didn't object when she refilled his glass and later opened another bottle. They talked about the village school and Mary's kindness and life in White Bircham.

Driving home was the last thing on his mind as Anna put the empty bottle and the remains of the second one on the draining board.

'That was delicious,' she said. 'Thank you.'

'Thank you.' He grinned. She picked up the empty Chinese food cartons and staggered slightly.

'Whoops,' she said, giggling. 'Red wine. Always makes me dizzy if I drink too much and more than one glass is too much. What was I thinking?'

'I've got to go,' Mac said, getting to his feet and feeling as if his knees had turned to hot liquid. Wine didn't normally have that effect — nor did being with an attractive woman for that matter. 'Oh, hell.'

'Hell?'

He dangled his car keys from his finger. He had a rule never to drive after drinking and being tired, the alcohol would have an even more potent effect on him. But he'd known he had to drive home, so why hadn't he objected when she kept filling his glass? And why had she filled it over and over unless . . . unless she wanted him to stay.

'Ah,' she said and then she giggled again. It seemed to startle her. She covered her mouth as if she'd done something wrong, but she couldn't stifle the laughter. She looked at him with wide shocked eyes and burst out laughing again, then got herself under control. 'Sorry. Not funny. You can sleep here if you like.'

His eyebrows rose. Stay here. With her. Sleep under the same roof. Even if that was what she meant, he couldn't take her up on it, couldn't trust himself.

He laughed at the craziness of it, but she was no longer laughing. She was regarding him closely with those serious green eyes and the little line between her eyebrows had deepened.

'Unless of course there's somewhere you'd rather be,' she said quickly. 'Um, I mean have to be.'

'There's nowhere in the world . . . ' he began, feeling himself unravel a little more, knowing, just knowing they were going to spend the night together. 'Look, I can get a taxi.'

'And then have to come out here to pick up your car tomorrow?' she said. 'If the prospect of sleeping on my sofa is so awful . . . '

'Your sofa.' He laughed.

She laughed, too, much to his relief.

'Did you think I was going to offer you my bed?'

His silence in answer to her question told her everything she needed to know. *What are you doing?* The voice of Common Sense, of Anna Curtis, of everything she had lived and worked for, shouted at her. But she was sick of listening to that voice, sick of putting on a brave face, of being strong and always doing the right thing. Would the world end if she did the wrong thing just this once?

'What if I did?' he asked huskily, his eyes smouldering. 'Would you be offended?'

Offended? That this gorgeous guy might have mistaken her invitation to stay the night as something else? That he might even be pleased about that? *This gorgeous guy*, Common Sense reminded her sternly, *is your new boss. You've* only known him since yesterday. Anna had never done anything reckless in her life. Everything she did, every move she made was carefully thought out and planned and consequences were always considered. And just how many opportunities had she missed in life because she was busy worrying about the consequences?

'Depends,' she murmured, moving closer to him so that she could smell the masculine scent of his body and breathe it in so it filled her senses.

This wasn't the wine talking. It wasn't the raw emotion of the day or the knock-on effects of tiredness kicking in. He looked every bit as confused and concerned as she felt, but there was something else blazing in those beautiful blue eyes of his and it certainly wasn't concern that he might be about to do something he may well regret in the morning.

He reached out, cradling her cheek in the palm of his hand so she could feel the heat radiating out of him. His touch sparked against her skin, sent frantic messages along her nerve ends.

He lowered his head and she moved closer still, their lips inches apart, centimetres, millimetres . . . She could taste the wine on his breath, feel the heat of his lips close to hers. It was now or never. She must stop this, must regain control, they'd regret it in the morning . . .

Their lips touched and there was no going back.

6

Mac woke before Anna. She was still in his arms. He couldn't recall a time when he'd ever felt as happy as this, or experienced this overwhelming feeling of utter contentment.

He slid his arms from around her and quietly got out of bed, leaving her to sleep on.

Her kitchen was neat and tidy and it wasn't difficult to find what he needed to make coffee.

He didn't hear her coming up behind him, didn't know she was there until he heard a soft sigh.

'Morning,' she said and yawned. He turned round and moved towards her, but she moved away giving him a wary look that reminded him of a trapped animal. That look made his heart tighten until it felt like a hard cold ball in his chest.

'Morning. Coffee's almost ready,' he said lightly.

'Great.'

She looked at the solitary mug standing on the side.

'Aren't you having one?'

'No time,' he said. 'I have to get home, get showered and changed and ready for work.'

'You can shower here,' she said.

'No, I can't,' he said. 'If anyone sees me leaving . . . '

For a moment she looked hurt, then her expression froze.

'Hey, I didn't mean it like that. You haven't even joined the practice yet and I don't want you being the subject of gossip from the word go. We'll keep this between ourselves for now, at least until you've settled in.'

He hoped she could see the logic in that.

'This?' she fired at him. 'This?'

'No,' he said, his frown matching hers. 'You know that's not what I mean, Anna. There's more to this, to us, than that.'

'We'd had too much to drink,' she said.

'No, Anna . . . '

'I'm giving you an out here, Mac,' she said. 'You can either take it or leave it. We can't be more than work colleagues. We both know that.'

Her eyes glittered with determination. He realised that standing here, arguing the toss with her, would get him nowhere, but he wasn't going to give up. For now he'd make a tactical withdrawal, give her the space she so clearly needed. It was all he could do.

'All right,' he murmured. 'We'll do things your way, Anna, but if you change your mind, I'll be waiting. You and I both know that we've got something special here and when you're ready . . . you just have to say the word. But in the meantime, I'll respect your wishes.'

He smiled and her shoulders sagged a little. He thought she may be about to give in, but she squared up, lifting her chin to speak.

'I won't change my mind, Mac.'

And she sounded as if she meant it.

★ ★ ★

Anna stood at the front door watching him drive away. Already it felt as if last night didn't happen, as if she'd dreamt the whole thing.

What a disastrous start. How on earth had she allowed things to go so far, to get so out of hand? She could have ruined everything.

He called in later in the day on his way back from the hospital, or so he said, even though Anna knew he would have had to make a detour to get here. He stayed for an hour, playing with Cameron in the back garden, filling Anna in on Gavin's progress.

Anna watched him, her heart aching. She wanted him so badly. She wondered if he really felt the same. When she saw him out, he kissed Cameron's cheek and made no move to kiss her.

'I'm on call every night for the rest of

the week,' he said regretfully. 'I don't think I'll be able to get back to see you.'

'Good,' she said coolly. 'You aren't under any obligation to me, Mac.'

'I know,' he said, smiling. 'I do understand where you're coming from, Anna, and I respect that.'

But he couldn't possibly understand and she couldn't tell him. Anna Curtis would never, could never, find it in herself to trust anyone.

On Saturday, when Anna was to move into Mary's cottage, she arranged to leave Cameron with Sandra, the child-minder. It would give them chance to get to know each other.

Her foot was much better and driving only caused a twinge.

She hadn't seen Mac since Tuesday. He'd phoned a couple of times to update her on Gavin, who had been quite poorly, but he hadn't come near Bircham Parva.

Anna had expected there to be tears when she left Cameron with Sandra, at the very least a woeful expression, but

Cameron had spotted the toys Sandra had ready for him and hurried off to investigate.

'I've got to go now, sweetie,' she said. 'But I'll be back soon.'

He cast her a look that almost said, 'Hurry up and go,' then he gave her a small wave as if to speed her departure before turning back to a large red tractor he'd spotted among the toys.

'Go,' Sandra urged when she saw the bewildered look in Anna's eyes. 'Just be thankful that he isn't kicking up hell and making a fuss. He'll be fine with me and when you're settled in with Mary, just come back for him.'

As she stumbled away from Sandra's house, she couldn't stop the tears. It was such a wrench leaving Cameron. She hadn't expected it to be so hard, but it was something she was going to have to get used to over the coming months — and years. Their lives were moving on, Cameron would have new people in his life. At first Sandra, then later nursery school teachers and onwards to primary school and before she knew it he'd be a teenager, maybe off to university or . . . She felt a gut-wrenching tug at her heart. Or he might end up like Christa.

'No,' she said, gritting her teeth and rubbing her eyes with a soggy tissue. 'That is not going to happen. No way. I won't let it.'

She headed for Mary's cottage and found the older woman waiting for her. She gave Anna a hug, then said, 'Come and see what we've done.'

Anna followed her into the cottage and was amazed at how empty it looked. All Mary's china and glass had gone, all her pictures removed from the walls and there was a faint smell of paint.

'You've decorated?' Anna whispered.

'Not me,' Mary said, smiling all over her face. 'Mac. He's worked so hard. He's been covering nights as well. When he took the pictures down to move them into the annexe, there were light patches left on the walls. He said he couldn't leave it like that and the next thing I knew, he was driving me to that big DIY store and getting me to choose paint.' She broke off and peered at Anna. 'Have you been crying?'

'It was leaving Cameron,' Anna admitted with a rueful smile. 'I don't know what got into me. It's so silly.'

'Oh, dear. Was he terribly upset at being left?'

'Actually, he wasn't upset at all. He couldn't wait for me to leave.'

'Well, you can get different curtains if you wish, and there's room if you want to buy any furniture of your own, but you're welcome to use all of this. And if you don't like the colour we chose . . . '

'I love the colour, Mary.' Anna laughed.

'Ah, you started without me!'

Anna spun round and gasped. Mac.

* * *

How come Mac could look so gorgeous while just wearing jeans and a white

T-shirt? How was she going to cope with the reality of seeing him every day? The only way to keep her feelings hidden would be to act cool, keep her smiles tight and try not to be drawn into his beautiful eyes.

'Hi,' she said. Friendly but cool. Good.

'Hi.' He grinned at her and, almost at once, she nearly came undone.

Mary said nothing, but looked from one to the other of them with a bemused smile as if she couldn't quite believe what her eyes were telling her. The way they were looking at each other was a dead giveaway — something was going on between them.

'I'm free to give you a hand today,' Mac said. 'So I'm all yours.'

'It's kind of you, but there's really no need,' Anna said quickly, desperate to avert a possible disaster. 'You've already done so much this week.'

But he wasn't taking no for an answer.

'I'll give you a hand emptying your

car and then I'll drive you back to Bircham Parva for the rest of your stuff. Is there much more to come?'

'It's very kind of you. I think a couple of trips should do it,' Anna said. 'But I can take my car, too . . . '

'Drive back and forth with a painful foot?' Mac's eyebrows rose. 'I don't think so. And on that subject, I don't want you doing any home visits for a month. I'll handle those at first, okay?'

She knew it made sense and nodded her agreement.

With his help, her car was unpacked in double quick time and when they'd finished, she climbed into his car beside him. It was a different car this time, a big off-roader with plenty of boot space.

'This is very kind . . . ' she began.

'Please, Anna,' he husked, his eyes creasing with pain. 'I know this is difficult, but if you tell me how kind I am once more I think I'm going to go mad. I'm not doing this to be kind, I'm doing it because . . . '

She stared at him, horrified. Surely he wasn't going to start making declarations of love? Not when she couldn't blame it on the wine.

'Because you're a colleague and a friend and I'd do the same if it was Mary moving or even Martin. Okay? No strings, no ulterior motives I promise. I'm just doing a favour for a mate.'

'In that case, thank you, Mac.'

She smiled a wobbly smile, but it was the best she could manage.

At the cottage, Mac carried the boxes Anna had packed out to his car and when he'd loaded it up, he found her in the bedroom shaking pillows out of their cases.

'I forgot to strip the bed,' she said. 'The linen's mine. I'm not stealing it.' Why had she said that? It was the kind of defensive remark her sister would have made. She tried to laugh it off, but Mac was giving her a puzzled look.

'You're a very complicated girl, Anna,' he said, then he looked at the bed. Anna's cheeks burned. Her throat felt dry.

'I'll wait in the car,' he said, a pained look on his face. 'If you need a hand carrying anything else out, give me a shout, but I can't be here with you, Anna . . . ' He turned on his heel and pounded down the stairs.

Minutes later she hurried out to the car, fresh and confident, the last of her belongings in a couple of large black sacks, her composure restored.

She'd locked the door of the cottage for the last time. The cottage where she'd nursed Christa. As she tossed the key in her hand she felt she'd drawn a line under that chapter of her life. She was starting now with a clean sheet.

'Feel sad about leaving?' Mac asked as she fastened her seat belt.

'Why should I?'

'Because I'd guess you went through quite a lot with your sister here over the past few months.'

How did he do it? He seemed to have this ability to get right inside her and touch the things that hurt the most. But when she looked at his face, all she saw written there was concern.

'I do feel a little sad,' she admitted.

'If you need a hug . . . '

'I do not need a hug,' she said firmly, but she did. Her life had been lacking in hugs and she really could use one right now, but if she let Mac put his arms around her who knew where it might lead and she had to be strong, for Cameron's sake. For Christa.

'How about talking then?' Mac said gently. 'I'm a good listener.'

Anna bit her lip. There were things she'd never even told Fiona, things she'd never told anyone, but those things had been haunting her lately.

'Mac, I . . . '

'It may help. You look so sad, Anna, as if there's so much grief inside you. Would it really hurt you to try to let some of it out?'

She nodded, fastened her hands together in her lap and looked down at them. It seemed strange to be finally about to tell someone about her life sitting in a car stuffed to the roof with her belongings.

'How long have you got?' she joked, but the laughter didn't quite make it to her eyes.

'As long as you need.'

There was plenty she could tell him, but if she started at the beginning, they'd be here all day. Right now the hurt was all about Christa.

'I was twenty-four when Christa turned sixteen,' she began. 'She was allowed to move in with me then and I was so happy . . . ' she broke off, smiling, remembering how thrilled she'd been the day that Christa came home. But instead of a happy, relieved young woman, Anna had found herself landed with an angry and volatile teenager. She'd expected too much of her. She'd expected the sullen girl she used to visit at the home to suddenly turn into a happy-go-lucky young woman the minute she got out, but the hurt was too deep by then.

103

'I had such plans for her — for us,' Anna went on. 'But she blamed me for not getting her out of care sooner, but I couldn't have done it sooner, Mac, not if I was going to make any kind of life for us.'

'That must have hurt,' Mac said.

'Yes,' she whispered. 'All I wanted to do was provide my little sister with the stable home she had missed. She left home. She came back. She moved in with a man old enough to be her father, then moved back in with me again when it finally went wrong.' A deep sigh shuddered through her.

'And while all this was going on, you were trying to build your career,' Mac said. 'That can't have been easy without any parental support. Hell, it isn't easy when you've got that support.'

Anna had never looked at it like that before. She'd simply seen her life and her career as hers to work at, to get right.

'It wasn't easy for Christa either. It wasn't her fault — any of it. She had a tough time in care. I should have got her out sooner.'

'So you were supposed to do that as well as building a solid, secure future for both of you? You were looking at the future, Anna. Under the circumstances, I'd say that was a pretty mature thing to do.'

Mature or not, it had had a devastating effect on Christa's life.

'Just over two years ago, Christa came back for the last time. Pregnant. She wanted to have a termination, but I talked her out of it. Even then I wasn't sure I was doing the right thing. What hope for Christa's child when she was a drug user?'

Mac shook his head.

'Are you sure you want to hear this?' Anna said doubtfully.

'Yes, go ahead,' he said supportively. 'I want to hear it, Anna.'

'When I looked at Christa, I didn't see a thin, black-eyed girl with sores around her mouth, but a little frightened three-year-old huddled in the corner of the lounge, clutching her knees against her chin. That's how she was when I . . . when I came home from school and found our mother dead.'

Anna's voice finally cracked. That hug he'd offered earlier . . . she could use it now. She looked up at him, eyes steeped in misery.

'Oh, Anna,' Mac said raggedly.

'I wish you'd known Christa after Cameron was born,' Anna burst out. 'She changed. Oh, Mac, she really did change. Maternal love softened her. She wanted to be the best mother she could be and I was there to help her. For the first time in her life someone was dependant on her, someone helpless and defenceless, someone she could really love. It brought out the best in her and then . . . she got ill.'

'Aplastic anaemia,' Mac said, recalling the day of the marathon which now seemed a lifetime ago.

'At first I thought her extreme tiredness was due to her poor health during pregnancy. Then the physical signs started manifesting themselves.'

She broke off, the memory hurting more than she imagined possible. She'd blocked all this out, had dealt with her sister's illness a day at a time.

'I organised tests.'

She remembered those results exactly. They had been devastating.

'She had to have blood transfusions and then the diagnosis was made. Her only hope was a bone marrow transplant with me as the donor. Being Christa's sibling the chance of a match was good, but there was no match. My sister and I had different fathers neither of whom gave a damn about either of us. My father had abandoned me, leaving me in the care of a woman who didn't care. Then Christa's father did the same.'

'Your mother died, Anna,' Mac said softly. 'You can't blame her for . . . '

'Our mother was a drunk, Mac. I vowed I'd be better than that and yet I could see my sister going the same way and it tore me apart. But when she held Cameron in her arms for the first time, I knew . . . knew that she would never be like our mother, that she would be a good mother. All she needed was the chance to prove it.

'But Christa's years of drug and alcohol abuse had weakened her body and she was unable to fight back. All she ever got was breathing space before one treatment failed and another was tried.'

'What about Cameron's father?'

'He did a disappearing act the minute he found out Christa was pregnant,' Anna flashed. 'Just like my father, just like her father. It seems my sister was as terrible at choosing men as our mother. But my mother made the mistake of shutting everyone out. She had no friends, and no one seemed to care about her. Perhaps if someone had been there for her, she wouldn't have . . . wouldn't have died all alone on her kitchen floor.'

At least that was something. Christa

hadn't died alone. Anna had been with her, holding her hand as she passed. That was the only consolation.

'I don't want to make the same mistakes my mother did,' Anna said, a note of desperation creeping into her voice. 'I don't want to make the wrong decisions, put my trust in the wrong people. I've seen where it ends. I've seen the damage it can do.'

7

Mac reeled. He'd expected her to tell him about her sister's death and the way it had affected her. If only he'd known this sooner. No wonder Anna was so terrified of commitment.

'Anna I'm so sorry,' he said. 'I had no idea.'

'Of course you didn't,' she said. 'I've told you more than I've ever told anyone. Even Fiona doesn't know all the circumstances of our lives. It's not really the kind of thing you tell anyone . . . ever.'

'It's nothing to be ashamed of.'

'I'm not ashamed. But now you know,' she said and flashed him a quick smile. 'Shall we get on?'

They made small talk in the car. Mac wondered if she regretted telling him all that, but it was too late for regrets. He knew and somehow that made everything different. It was time to stop acting like a lovesick idiot and start behaving like the responsible adult he was supposed to be.

When they got back to Mary's, Mac helped unload the car and declined Mary's offer of dinner.

'Well,' Mary huffed when he'd gone. 'That's a first. I've never known Mac turn down a free meal in his life.'

Anna knew why he'd done it and she was grateful.

Later that night, Anna looked out of her funny little bedroom window. It had been a busy day and an emotional one, but talking to Mac had been therapeutic and in a strange way she felt as if a weight had been lifted from her shoulders.

Cameron had been delighted to see her and relieved to be going home even though he insisted on giving Sandra a kiss and a big goodbye hug. He didn't seem to notice that home was different. His familiar things were arranged about his room and Anna had hung his *Balamory* curtains at the window.

Anna crept into his room before going to bed herself and covered him up. She stroked his cherubic face, her heart swelling with love for him. Somehow she was going to make up to this little boy for all the things his poor mother had suffered.

'Oh, bed, glorious bed,' she murmured as she sank into the soft mattress and buried her head in fat feather pillows.

* * *

The weekend passed in a blur and all too soon it was Monday.

Anna drove into the surgery car park just after Martin. He gave her a curt nod then entered the building, leaving the door to swing shut in her face. In fact, it would have hit her if a hand hadn't come from behind her and slammed into it, pushing it open again.

'Sorry about him,' Mac said tightly. 'My cousin must have left his manners at home this morning.'

'It doesn't worry me, Mac,' Anna said. 'I'm so happy to be here and looking forward to getting started, no one can spoil it for me.'

'That's the spirit.' He grinned. 'Good luck. Any problems, let me know. Mary will look after you.'

Mary was waiting to settle Anna into her room like a teacher settling a child for her first day at school.

'You've got half an hour before your first appointment,' Mary said. 'And make sure you keep your foot elevated. I've put a cushion on the chair for you to put your foot on.'

As first days go, Anna's went extremely well.

One week merged into another. Mac was friendly, but kept his distance and Anna wasn't sure if he was doing it out of kindness because he felt sorry for her, or because, despite what he'd said, he somehow thought less of her.

After a month Mac said she could start making house calls.

'Mac's waiting for you in reception,'

Mary said. 'He's going to share home visits with you until you get a feel for the area. It shouldn't take long.'

'There's no need,' Anna said. 'I've got my sat-nav.'

'No, really,' Mary said. 'Some of the roads out here are little more than tracks. Mac will be able to show you which to avoid and which to use as short cuts. We get a lot of trees down around here in winter and it's good to know some alternative routes.'

'Okay.' Anna smiled.

'Are you ready for this?' Mac asked, his tone friendly, his smile practically knocking her off her feet when they headed for the car park.

'I can't wait. Once I'm doing house calls, I'll feel like a genuine member of the team.'

'But you are a genuine member of the team,' he said with a puzzled grin.

'I know, but I want to pull my weight, Mac.'

He pointed his key at his car and the doors unlocked with a friendly little bleep. Their sleeves brushed as they walked over and they sprang apart.

'Whoops!' Mac grinned. 'We're going to have to stop overreacting like that, aren't we?'

'We will,' Anna said, heart pounding in her throat. 'Our circumstances are a bit unusual, that's all. We'll get used to it. It's not as if we had a relationship or anything. It was just the one night.'

'Yes, that's all it was. I'll drive and you can look round, check out the terrain. I'm going to show you Cow Lane. It's a great short cut to the old houses behind the new estate, but the gritters don't go down there in winter so it's not one to be used in icy conditions or you'll end up in the ditch.'

'Spoken like one who knows?' Anna said.

'Well, I ended up wrapped round a tree and my bike landed in the ditch, but, yes, it is the voice of experience you hear. And one thing I know is that I will never get on that bike again.'

'You had an accident?' Anna said.

'My own fault,' he said ruefully. 'I was on my way to an emergency, but the gossips will have it that I was deliberately driving recklessly, trying to kill myself because my wife had left me.'

'I'm sorry,' she murmured.

'Why? Because my wife left me or because people like to gossip?'

'Both,' she said. And she was sorry. Mac should be married. He should have a devoted, loving wife and several children, probably a dog, too. He was a good guy. His wife must have been crazy to leave him.

He laughed.

'It's an occupational hazard of being a GP in a small country practice. Everyone knows you and they think they know your business. You get used to it. There's plenty of speculation about you.'

'Me?'

'They mean well, Anna. Don't take their curiosity the wrong way. When

116

they get to know you, they'll take you to their hearts just like . . . ' he broke off and blinked. 'Just like we all have,' he finished.

'Thank you.' She smiled.

'I know you're not technically Cameron's mother, but to all intents and purposes you are a single mother. It's got to be tough on you.'

She stared at him, unsure of quite where the conversation was going.

'Are you having second thoughts about employing a single mother?'

'Of course not!' He laughed. 'I'm trying to be supportive and not doing a very good job of it.'

'You're doing a great job,' she murmured huskily. 'I'm glad to have you as a friend.' She turned to look out of the window before he saw in her glistening eyes that he meant so much more to her than that.

'Here we are, first call,' he said, pulling up outside a pair of lonely cottages. 'Hilda Briggs. Her neighbour, Ted Seaman called me this morning.

He says she's sitting in her kitchen glaring at him, but she won't let him in. Frankly I don't blame her. Ted's a stranger to soap and water, but it's not like Hilda to be unsociable although she can be stubborn.'

'You know her well?'

'She used to be my school teacher and my Sunday school teacher. I wouldn't say I knew her well, but she probably knows me better than anyone.'

They got out of the car and a small man in dirty clothes scuttled out to greet them.

'Am I glad to see you, Mac,' Ted said. 'There's no change. She's still sat there staring at me.'

'It's all right, Ted,' Mac said. 'We'll handle things now. I'll call in after I've seen Hilda and let you know what's happening.'

'Who's that?'

'Doctor Curtis, Ted,' Mac said. 'She's joined the practice.'

'Oh,' Ted's wrinkled old face fell. 'I thought you'd got yourself a pretty young girlfriend.'

'I should be so lucky,' Mac muttered under his breath. 'Go and make yourself a cup of tea, Ted. I'll see you in a minute.'

With an exaggerated wink at Anna accompanied by a toothless smile, Ted hurried back into his own cottage.

While Mac searched for a key in the back garden, Anna looked in through the window. She saw what was the unmistakable aftermath of a stroke.

'We're going to need an ambulance, Mac,' she said. Hilda Briggs was sitting in a fireside chair. She wasn't glaring, she was staring.

'Make the call, Anna,' Mac said as he found the key and plunged it into the deadlock on the back door. 'Then get the oxygen.'

She reached for her phone while Mac rushed in and straight across to the woman. She was still in her nightdress. Anna watched her face light slightly at the sight of him.

'Hello, Hilda,' Mac said. 'It's Mac.

Can you see me?'

'Course I can see you,' Hilda spluttered. Although her words were slightly slurred, it was possible to hear what she was saying. 'I'm not blind.'

Anna made the call for an ambulance and fetched oxygen from the car. Mac put the mask over Hilda's face and she immediately tried to pull it off.

'What are you doing?' she demanded.

'Hilda, you've had a stroke,' Mac said. 'The oxygen will help and then we're going to get you to hospital — to the new stroke unit — and . . . '

'No!' Hilda shouted. 'What about chickens? What about Ted? Riordan McKenna, don't you touch me,' Hilda said angrily as Mac attempted to take her blood pressure.

'I'm your doctor, Hilda,' Mac said raggedly. His eyes reflecting the pain he felt inside.

Anna pressed her hand on his shoulder, gently moving him aside.

'Mac,' she murmured. 'Let me.'

He turned to look at her, his eyes

rimmed with red.

'Anna, she's in her nightclothes,' he whispered. 'She could have been sitting there like that for hours. It may even have happened during the night.'

'There's nothing we can do about that. The ambulance is on the way and she'll go straight to the stroke unit. They'll assess her there and decide on appropriate treatment.'

'Who's that?' Hilda cried.

'This is Doctor Curtis, Hilda,' Mac said and Anna moved round into Hilda's line of vision.

'Miss Briggs to you, young man!' Hilda corrected him.

'I haven't called her Miss Briggs for years,' he murmured. He seemed lost. 'I'm sorry, Miss Briggs. I'm a doctor now, I . . .'

'Your father is a doctor,' Hilda said and he gave Anna a look of utter despair. Strokes were vile things, bewildering for the sufferers and baffling for their loved ones. There was obviously a lot of affection between

121

Mac and Hilda and she could see that seeing her like this was hurting him. She knew his mother had died when he was young and suspected that, along with Mary, Hilda had been a sort of surrogate mother to him.

'Mac, why don't you pop next door and talk to Ted, ask him what time he first noticed Hilda sitting in her chair,' Anna said calmly. 'Ask if he saw her out and about at all this morning, feeding her hens or hanging out washing, anything like that. Then call Mary and find out exactly when he called the surgery to request the home visit.'

Mac smiled.

'Thanks, Anna,' he said. 'Thank goodness one of us is thinking clearly.'

'Little devil,' Hilda said. 'Don't bother poor old Mr Seaman . . . '

Little! Mac was way over six feet tall, but to Hilda he was a child.

Anna turned back to Hilda.

'Now, then,' Anna said briskly. 'How much do you understand of what I'm saying Miss Briggs?'

'Call me Hilda.'

'All right, Hilda.' Anna smiled. 'And please call me Anna. An ambulance is coming to take you to hospital. There's a specialist stroke unit there where you will get the best treatment. I know you're worried about your hens and Ted, but I'll see they're taken care of, I promise, okay?'

'All right,' Hilda said compliantly.

'I'm just going to check your blood pressure now and I want you to keep this oxygen mask on for a short while, could you do that for me?'

'Yes.'

The back door opened a few minutes later.

'Ambulance has arrived,' Mac said.

'Don't leave me,' she said to Anna.

'I won't,' Anna promised. 'I'll come in the ambulance with you.'

She turned to Mac.

'Ted says she was outside feeding the hens at nine o'clock this morning and she was fine then,' Mac said. 'Apparently they always have a cup of coffee at ten, but when he turned up she was just sitting in her chair and wouldn't let him in. Mary confirms that he called the surgery at ten-fifteen. So if you guys can get her to the hospital fast . . . '

'I'm going with her, Mac,' Anna said, touching his arm and giving him a reassuring smile. 'I'll let you know what happens.'

'Thanks, Anna. I'd better get in touch with her niece.'

Anna gave his arm a squeeze and this time he smiled.

'She'll be okay, Mac. And I'll be back for afternoon surgery. I told her I'd see that the hens and Ted were taken care of.'

'Ted's been watching out for her for years,' Mac murmured. 'But I'll make sure everything's okay here before I leave.'

★   ★   ★

Mac watched the ambulance drive away then turned to Ted who seemed to have shrivelled even more since the ambulance arrived.

'I don't like it,' Ted said. 'Her going to hospital. What if she doesn't ever come back?'

'They can do marvellous things these days,' Mac said.

'I thought she was dead,' Ted said, tears welling in his eyes. 'I honestly did. I was too scared to say it, but when I saw her, I thought she'd gone.'

Mac wouldn't admit it, but at first sight he'd thought so, too. And as the old man started to sob, Mac put his arm around his shoulders and led him back into his cottage. Whatever his own pain, he could probably at least double it in Ted's case.

When Ted had stopped crying, Mac asked him about the hens.

'Don't worry about them,' he said. 'I'll feed hers when I feed mine and I'll make sure they're all in at night. She's been forgetting to do it lately so I've been doing it for her now and then.'

'Forgetting?'

'Now take that look off your face young Mac,' Ted said. 'It's old age. Comes to us all. You get a bit forgetful. You must remember she's in her eighties now. Anyway, what about that girl you had with you?'

'What about her?'

'Well if you ask me, she'd make a nice little wife for you. The other one was . . . well, a nice enough girl, but not right for you.'

'I didn't ask you, Ted,' Mac said, but he couldn't stop a smile spreading across his face. No one in the village had approved of his choice of wife and as it turned out, they were probably right.

'Will you let me know when there's news?' Ted asked.

'Of course I will,' Mac said. 'I'll call by this evening after surgery.'

Outside in his car, Mac took out his mobile phone. It had always been at the back of his mind that one day he'd have to make this call and he had Hilda's niece's number in the phone's memory.

His mouth felt dry as he waited for her to answer.

'Abigail? Hi, it's Mac.'

There was a few seconds of silence.

'Mac . . . what is it?' Her voice was tight, unfriendly. 'What do you want?'

'How are you?'

Another silence.

'You haven't spoken to me since the divorce, so I know you haven't called to ask after my health, Mac,' she said waspishly.

'It's Hilda,' he said, knowing there was no easy way to break the news. 'I'm afraid she's had a stroke and she's been taken to the stroke unit . . . '

'A stroke? Aunt Hilda? But she's as strong as an ox!'

Mac bit back the comment that maybe Hilda had been as strong as an ox when Abigail last saw her over two years ago. But wasn't he to blame for Abigail's long absence? No, he wouldn't take the blame for that. He might have been able to shoulder the blame for the break up of their marriage, but there was absolutely nothing that was stopping Abi from visiting Hilda.

'How bad is she?'

'Hard to tell at the moment,' Mac said. 'I can call you when she's been assessed, or . . . '

'I'll come down,' she said quickly. 'I want to see her.'

'I'm sorry, Abi,' he murmured.

'Yes, well.' She sighed. 'I guess we've all moved on since I was last in the village. Contact me if there's any change, but I'll be making my way there as soon as I can.'

She didn't say making her way home. She'd never felt as if the village were home and that had been part of the problem. They met as children when Abigail came to stay with Hilda in the school holidays. She'd always loved coming to the village and had tried to settle in as Mac's wife, but after a while she began to hate the restrictions of her life.

Perhaps Mac could have saved their marriage if he'd been willing to go on giving her everything she wanted, but the fact was that when it came to a choice, there was no choice and he'd let Abi go.

He tossed his phone down onto the passenger seat, checked where else he had to go on his rounds this morning then set off, his heart heavy for too many reasons to count.

8

At the hospital, Hilda was taken straight to the stroke assessment unit. There was something very dignified about Hilda. She clutched Anna's hand when the blood taker came to take blood. The woman smiled at Anna.

Hilda squeezed Anna's hand and managed a wobbly, lop-sided smile.

Anna waited in the ward while Hilda was taken for an MRI scan and stayed with her until she'd got the results.

She would have preferred to stay with Hilda until her niece arrived, but she still had to find her way back to the village and get back to work.

Before she left she picked up a few things from the hospital shop. A bottle of squash, some fruit, tissues and a potted plant, but it would remind Hilda that she wasn't alone and she was being thought about.

She checked that Hilda had her emergency button to hand so that she could summon a nurse if needed, then kissed her forehead lightly.

'Let them look after you, Hilda,' she said softly. 'I'll come back and see you later.'

She had a lump in her throat the size of a tennis ball as she hurried away.

Outside the hospital, Anna went to the bus stop to check the timetable.

'Anna.'

She'd been unaware of the car slowing down and looked round sharply.

'Mac!'

'How is she?'

'They confirmed an ischaemic stroke,' she replied. 'And she seemed quite settled when I left.'

'Are you going to get in?'

'You didn't come all this way to give me a lift did you?'

'Well, I could tell you I was passing, but I don't think you'd believe me.'

'Did you contact her niece?' Anna asked as she got into the car.

131

'Actually, she's her great-niece,' he said. Did she imagine it, or did his eyes cloud slightly. 'Yes, I did. She's on her way.'

'Good,' Anna said.

'Maybe,' Mac said softly. 'What time's your first patient?'

'Four o'clock.'

'Same here. Would you like to have a late lunch? We have an hour. I've got some eggs in the fridge — I could attempt an omelette.'

'Actually,' Anna said. 'I'm starving. That would be great — thanks.'

Home was the big house in Grange Road. The kitchen was huge — a dream of a room for anyone who loved to cook. Anna watched as he opened the enormous American style fridge. There was barely anything in it.

Why on earth would a single man live in a huge house like this? She looked through the window at a garden that should be filled with children.

'Did you live here with your wife?'

'Ex-wife,' he said. 'No, I didn't. We

132

were in the process of buying it when we split up.'

He started breaking eggs into a bowl, bashing them on the edge a little harder than he needed to.

'Let me. Where's your omelette pan?'

'I don't know.' He shrugged helplessly.

'You really are hopeless.' She laughed and found a set of frying pans that looked as if they'd never been used.

This was yet another facet to Mac, this look of vulnerability when his hair flopped forward and he got that slightly bemused look in his eyes.

'Chop up that tomato,' she said briskly. 'It'll make it a bit more interesting. And you could grate some cheese to put on the top.'

'Let's see,' he said. 'For that I'd need a grater.' He looked round at the cupboards and drawers as if he'd never seen them before.

'I thought you were joking,' she said. 'You must have a grater somewhere.'

'Well, yes,' he said, clearly frustrated.

'Abi used to grate cheese . . . '

'That would be Abi, your ex-wife — the one that didn't live here?'

'Right,' he said distractedly. 'She let me keep all the kitchen utensils and equipment. I think it was her idea of a joke.'

The cooker was spotless She wouldn't mind betting it was never used.

'That looks absolutely delicious,' Mac said. 'I'm going to have to invite you for lunch more often.'

Would it really be so terrible, Anna thought as she looked across the table at him, if I did allow myself to fall in love with Riordan McKenna? He's settled here, I want to settle here, what could go wrong?

They ate in companionable silence, then Mac silently loaded the dishwasher and they headed back to the surgery in his car.

'I'll call in and see Hilda tonight,' Mac said. 'I'll let you know if there's any news.'

'Thanks, Mac, I'd appreciate that.'

'I know.' He smiled, a soft, gentle smile. 'That's why I knew you'd be right for us.'

* * *

Anna had never felt so content, so settled, in her life. Cameron was positively thriving in Sandra's care. Life was good. And Hilda was astounding everyone with the speed of her recovery. Hilda's niece had moved in to Hilda's cottage, but from the whispering and muttering she'd heard, Anna got the impression that the niece was not a popular person.

And there was Mac, of course. Since things had settled down, a real friendship was beginning to develop between them, a friendship that deepened Anna's feelings towards him. She began to feel something she had rarely felt in her life before — Anna began to feel safe.

On Friday, after late surgery, Anna saw Mac heading for his car.

'Mac,' she said, and when he turned, there was no hopeful look in his eye as there had been in the past. Maybe she'd done too good a job of convincing him that there could never be anything between them. She sighed. 'I'm planning to take Cameron to the forest for a picnic, and I wondered if . . . '

'Be careful if you do,' he said before she could continue. 'Stick to the marked paths and take a whistle with you so that if you do get lost you can use it to summon help.'

She blinked taken aback. Did he realise she was going to invite him along and was he saving her from making a fool of herself by asking? Could his feelings really have cooled off that much in a matter of days? Well, why not? They'd heated up faster than that in the first place, so why shouldn't they go off the boil just as quickly?

'Are you going to be seeing Hilda at the weekend?' she asked to cover her confusion.

'I expect so,' he said wearily. 'I

promised Ted I'd take him in to see her when I go.'

'I would have thought her niece . . . '

'She won't let Ted in her car,' he replied. 'I don't really blame her. Goodnight, Anna. Have a good week-end — and be careful in the forest.'

'I will,' she said, her throat contracting. She'd just been given the gentlest brush off ever, but none had ever hurt more.

*   *   *

Mac watched Anna walk away, watched the graceful way her body moved with every step. She didn't turn back. Oh, how it hurt to do that to her. How he would have loved to go into the forest with her, taking her to the special places that only locals knew, sharing his life, his world with her.

'Regretting taking her on?' Martin drawled as he emerged from the building. 'Now that circumstances have changed.'

'Not for a minute,' Mac said. 'She's the best thing that's happened round here for years. And I don't see how anything has changed.'

'Really? How is Abigail?' Martin asked pointedly. 'I heard she was back.'

'I wouldn't know,' Mac said, his jaw tightening, his cheek twitching. 'I haven't seen her, either.'

Martin looked genuinely surprised.

'I thought you two would be . . . well, you know.'

'No, I don't know, Martin,' Mac said coldly and got into his car before he caved in and gave Martin the satisfaction of losing his temper.

He drove to his father's house. Patrick was cooking.

'I've made spaghetti Bolognese,' Patrick said when Mac walked in.

The food smelled delicious. Mac realised the last time he'd eaten well was when Anna made him the omelette. The rest of the week had been microwaveable ready meals from the freezer.

'I see Hilda is doing well,' Patrick

said and Mac knew where this was leading. 'I called in to see her last night.'

'Yes, she's a remarkable woman,' Mac said.

'Abigail was there. She says she hasn't seen you yet.'

'There's no reason she should have done.'

'Except you were married,' Patrick said wryly.

'And bitterly divorced,' Mac added. 'I should think I'm the last person she wants to see.'

'It wasn't the impression I got,' Patrick said. 'But she really didn't fit in here did she? She never felt at home. You should have married . . . '

'A nice local girl,' Mac finished for him. 'Yes, I know.'

'It isn't too late.'

'Dad . . . ' Mac began, then he sighed.

'So what about Abigail?' Patrick said when they sat down to eat.

'What about her?'

'Are you going to see her?'

'I don't know, Dad. I don't suppose

she really wants to see me and I'm not going to chase around after her. Now can we close the subject, please?'

'You can't put it off forever,' Patrick said.

Despite being faced with good food, Mac's appetite had vanished.

★　★　★

Mary insisted on helping Anna to pack her picnic the following morning.

'You should have invited Mac to go with you,' Mary said.

'I think he has plans for this weekend,' Anna said.

'Ah, yes, of course, I was forgetting,' Mary said. 'I expect he'll be spending some time with Abigail.'

'Abigail?'

'Yes, you know, Hilda's great-niece. She's Mac's ex-wife.'

'I see,' Anna said, forcing a smile.

'I'm sorry, dear, I thought you knew.' Mary gave a little laugh. 'Actually, if I'm honest, you fit in so well here that I sometimes forget you haven't always been around and don't know all there is to know about everyone.'

Anna smiled, grasped the handles of the buggy and headed for the forest.

It was deliciously cool under the canopy of trees and there was a never-ending supply of sights to enthrall Cameron. He squealed with delight every time he saw a dog and a few came over to the buggy and allowed him to pet them. A group of horse riders trotting past brought more yells of joy and when he saw a squirrel scamper up a tree and along a branch, he clasped his hands together and said, 'Wow!'

No wonder Mac had cooled off. All she knew of his marriage was that it had ended. She didn't know who had ended it or if it had been a mutual decision, but Abigail being back had unsettled him.

This just proved she had been right not to get involved with Mac.

'We'll stop here for our picnic, Cameron,' she said.

She smiled and reached for a sandwich, but the thought of eating anything gave her a nauseous feeling. She gulped back a gag. Strange. She'd felt like this yesterday around lunchtime and hadn't been able to eat. Yet she didn't feel ill. Apart from feeling tired, she felt fine.

*   *   *

The next day Anna had to go to the hospital and, while she was in town, she picked up a pregnancy testing kit and dropped it in her bag. *Just in case*, she thought. *Just to prove that I'm worrying about nothing.* While there, she popped in to see Hilda.

'How are you feeling?'

'A bit of a fraud really,' Hilda said. 'And guilty for getting Abigail all this way here for nothing when she's such a busy person.'

'I expect she wanted to see you anyway,' Anna said and Hilda gave a doubtful snort.

They were still chatting a few minutes later when Anna heard someone clear their throat behind her. She turned and knew that this was Abigail, Mac's ex-wife, without anyone having to tell her. She was tall and beautiful. No wonder Mac had lost interest in Anna if this was the alternative.

'You must be Doctor Curtis,' she said, smiling, the smile transforming her face, making it even prettier. 'I've been hoping to see you, to thank you for looking after Aunt Hilda that day. Mac said that you're the person I should be thanking.'

'Anna,' Anna said returning her smile.

'I was afraid . . . I . . . ' her bottom lip wobbled. Anna could see she was on the verge of tears and only just holding it together.

'Perhaps you'd like to walk me to the door,' Anna said quickly. 'Goodbye, Hilda. I'll come and see you again soon.'

She kissed Hilda's cheek then walked with Abigail to the end of the ward.

'Are you all right?' she said. 'You seem very upset.'

'It's just been so awful seeing Aunt Hilda like this.'

She couldn't stop the tears any longer. Anna put her arm around her and led her down the corridor to a quiet seating area.

'She's doing marvellously well,' Anna said. 'Really.'

'It's not just my aunt,' Abigail admitted. 'It's Mac. I suppose you know we were married . . .'

'I had heard,' Anna said.

'Seeing him at the weekend just brought it home what I'd lost,' she sobbed. 'If only I hadn't been so stubborn. I was so desperate to have a baby and I suppose I lost sight of what was important.'

Anna knew it was none of her business and it wasn't her place to ask, but she had to know. Her skin crawled with dread.

'Mac didn't want children?'

'No,' Abigail sniffed. 'He was dead

set against it. I don't know why because he seems to love kids — just not his own . . . I'm sorry — you didn't come here to listen to all my troubles.'

She dabbed carefully at her eyes. After all that, her make-up was still intact. There wasn't so much as a smudge.

So Mac loved kids — as long as they weren't his own. She thought of the pregnancy testing kit in her bag and bit hard on her lip. What on earth was she going to do if it was positive? How was it possible to be so happy about something, yet at the same time dread it with all your heart?

★ ★ ★

Anna waited until Cameron was asleep that evening before taking the pregnancy testing kit out of her bag and heading for the bathroom.

She sat on the edge of the bath, waiting for the result, her stomach tying itself in knots, her heart pounding. *Please let it be negative*, she begged.

'Oh,' she gasped seeing the little cross which indicated a positive result. She didn't know whether to laugh or cry. 'Oh, Christa! Do you see what I've done now?'

When Christa had come to her pregnant and upset, Anna had encouraged her to embrace the change in her life that this wonderful event would bring. She hadn't really understood how it felt to be pregnant, to have a life growing inside you, someone who would be wholly dependant on you. She hadn't understood how it felt to have all that and to face it alone.

'I'm sorry, Christa,' she murmured as tears slid down her cheeks. She'd already let Christa down. Now she and Cameron would have to move on, just when they were getting settled — there was no way she could stay here.

* * *

'Your resignation?' Mac paled as he looked at the letter Anna had just handed to him. 'Are you serious? Why, Anna?'

'Personal reasons,' she said.

He stared at her, but she was looking anywhere but at him.

'Sit down, Anna,' he said and she remained standing. 'Anna, sit down!'

She sat, perched on the edge of the chair as if ready to make a run for it. She looked pale, dark-eyed and, for the first time in a long time, those eyes wore that haunted expression he'd seen the first day he saw her.

'What's happened?' he asked gently.

She shook her head. 'I can't tell you that,' she said. 'I'm sorry, Mac. You've been so good to me — everyone here has, but I have to move on. I can stay until you find a suitable replacement . . . '

'It took me years to find you,' he said, his voice giving out on him, cracking as he fought with himself not to sound desperate. 'Anna, don't leave us. We can work this out between us, I know we can. I thought we were friends.'

'I can stay until Christmas,' she said resolutely, her voice not wavering at all. 'Then I must leave.'

Mac stood up and walked over to the window.

'I don't buy this, Anna,' he said. 'You and Christa chose this place together. This is where your sister wanted her son to grow up. When I first met you, you were determined to stick to that plan no matter what.'

He turned to face her and caught her by surprise. She was near to tears, confusion creasing her forehead, the line between her eyes deeper than he'd ever seen it.

He went to her, grasped her hands and held them in his.

'Don't do this, Anna. You've never run away from anything in your life — why start now?'

She heaved a sigh and looked at him, her green eyes pale with sorrow, shimmering with unshed tears. He pulled her towards him and she came out of the chair, into his arms weeping as she rested her head against his chest.

'Oh, Anna . . . ' He smoothed her hair and gently kissed her head. 'What is it, love? Can't you tell me?' he asked, the sorrow in his voice clear.

'No,' her reply was muffled by his shirt. He tightened his arms around her. If he could keep hold of her, as long as she was in his arms, he could stop her from leaving.

But he couldn't hold her forever. He couldn't stop her from leaving if that was what she really wanted. So why did he have the feeling that it wasn't what she wanted? What was he to do?

At last she pulled away from him, her face flushed and soaked with tears.

'I'm sorry,' she said.

He picked up her resignation and tore it to pieces, dropping it in the bin.

'I'll just write another,' she said.

'And I'll just tear it up,' he replied. 'Until you can give me a valid reason for your leaving, I'm not going to accept it, Anna. I think . . . no, scrub that, I *know* you're happy here and so is Cameron.'

'Sometimes,' she whispered, 'happiness is just not enough.'

9

Anna visited the surgery in town where she and Christa had registered as patients when they first moved to Bircham Parva. She wasn't going to leave her antenatal care to the last minute or to chance. She had a while before she had to be back at the surgery and made a detour to visit Ted. He was outside, sitting in the shade in an old folding chair, puffing on his pipe.

'Hello, Ted,' she said.

He got out of the chair and disappeared round the side of the house, appearing moments later with another chair which he set beside his.

'Sit yourself down.' He patted the seat of the chair. 'You look peaky.'

'Thanks.' She grinned as she sat on the rickety chair. 'How are you?'

'I'm fine,' he said. 'Better now *she's* gone.'

He turned his eyes to the house next door.

'Hilda?'

'No,' he said. 'Abigail.'

'She's gone?'

'Had to get back to work she said,' he muttered. 'Not that she told me. I heard her telling that fella.'

'What fella's that, Ted?'

'The one that came here with her,' Ted said. 'A right smarmy type. I knew he was in there eyeing up Hilda's stuff, seeing how much it's all worth. He wanted to come in here and look at my things and I wouldn't let him.'

'I didn't realise she was with anyone,' Anna murmured.

'Oh, yes,' Ted chuckled. 'She's never been without a man. That was half the problem when she was with Mac. One man was never enough . . . '

Anna said nothing. She didn't put too much store by what Ted said. He came out with some odd things and he'd made no secret of the fact he didn't like Abigail.

'She'll get her comeuppance, though,' Ted said. 'Hilda and I sold these cottages a while ago. We live here rent free until we die, then that's it. We've both got nice little nest eggs put by.'

'That sounds very sensible,' Anna said.

'We're not daft. We planned for our old age. We've never left anything to chance in our lives, no reason to start now. I heard them talking about pulling Hilda's place down, having something better built in its place, selling it on for a good price. They won't be able to do that.' He chuckled.

'No,' Anna said, feeling faintly disgusted with Abigail after her fake show of emotion at the hospital. 'They certainly won't.'

* * *

After seeing a few patients, Anna emerged from her surgery. Her mouth was filling again, her stomach tightening.

As she was passing Mac's room, his door opened and he came out, his face breaking into a genuine smile of pleasure.

'Anna! I was hoping to see you. Would you have lunch with me?'

'I can't,' she said. 'Sorry.'

'I don't expect you to cook,' he said and Anna gave him a horrified look that made him laugh. 'And I wasn't intending to cook, either, so you don't have to worry about being poisoned. We could go to the Green Man.'

'I really can't.' She wondered how long she could stand here before the urge to heave finally overwhelmed her.

'Yes, you can,' he said. 'Come on. No strings. Just lunch. I haven't eaten a proper meal for days. Look at me. I'm in danger of wasting away!'

'All right.' She grinned. 'But I don't want much.'

She thought she could handle it. Thought she'd be okay sitting with Mac while he ate, but the smell of his steak and the sight of his knife cutting through it was too much. She leapt from her seat and fled, just making it to the bathroom before the horrible dry heaving started.

She splashed cold water onto her burning cheeks and emerged from the bathroom, praying this was the end of it for today.

Mac was waiting at their table. His plate had gone and he was watching anxiously for her. He looked at her and her stomach flipped.

'Still think you're leaving?' he asked.

'Mac, don't . . . we agreed . . . '

'Maybe we did,' he murmured. 'But there wasn't a deadline then. I thought I had all the time in the world to wait for you, but you've moved the goalposts. I don't believe you want to go, Anna.'

'I've made up my mind,' she said, getting to her feet. He caught her hand as she made to walk past him, and looked up with those smouldering eyes.

'Was it something Abi said?' he asked and she recoiled as if she'd been slapped. 'I thought so. What did she tell you?'

'Nothing,' she said, flustered. If what Abigail had told her was true and she had no reason to suppose it wasn't, then how long before he put two and two together. He was good at solving puzzles, good at working things out. It wouldn't take him long.

'I'm not in love with her, Anna,' he said. 'Our marriage was over a long time before our divorce.'

'That's none of my business,' Anna said, pulling her hand away. 'I have to get back to the surgery. I've a lot of paperwork to catch up on.'

Her heart hammered as she made her way back to the surgery. It wasn't the paperwork she needed to get back to, but her room where she could lie down. The tiredness usually got her just after the sickness and if she could just snatch a few minutes sleep before afternoon surgery, she could get through it. She kicked off her shoes and got onto the bed, closing her eyes as the crushing, bone-aching weariness washed over her, aware only of her pounding heart gradually slowing down as her eyelids grew heavy.

★ ★ ★

Mac was about to follow Anna to her room when Mary called to him.

'It's about Anna,' she said, lowering her voice. 'I'm worried about her.'

'Aren't we all,' Mac growled. 'Go on.'

'Do you think she's got too much work on? Today is the first time she's taken her lunch break. She usually stays in her office and reckons she has piles of paperwork to do, but there's no evidence of that in the out tray.'

Mac frowned.

'That's not all,' Mary went on. 'She's not sleeping. I have to get up in the night and lately every time I do, I can hear her moving about in the cottage.'

'I'm working on it, Mary,' he said, glancing towards Anna's room.

He walked towards the door and knocked softly. No answer. Gently he eased the door open and at first he thought the room was empty and was about to shut the door when he noticed her bag discarded on her desk.

'Anna?'

He pushed the door fully open and saw her on the bed. She was sound asleep. He reached out to touch her, then thought better of it. She clearly needed the sleep, but why? She was an otherwise healthy young woman — or was she? He noticed the tiny bruise in the crook of her arm. Blood test?

He left her to sleep and returned to his own office. Her sister had died of bone marrow failure. Could there be a connection? An underlying genetic condition or disease, a link between the sisters? He felt sick to his stomach.

★ ★ ★

At the weekend, Anna set off with Cameron for another picnic in the forest. The weather had cooled and the forest smelled damp from rain.

Cameron was overawed as usual and

Anna hoped that having a younger child around wouldn't dampen his spirit. Leaning forward, she ruffled his hair and he squirmed round and looked up at her, grinning all over his face.

She walked further into the forest until they arrived at a rushing stream lit by the sun streaming through the trees. It was magical.

Cameron tucked in to Mary's home made quiche and cherry tomatoes, biting into the sweet fruit until juice ran down his chin. Anna nibbled on a piece of chicken waiting for the usual water springs to let her know her stomach was about to rebel. For a while she thought she was going to be able to eat, but soon the feeling washed over her.

After lunch, the tiredness closed in. Anna wrapped the handle of Cameron's reins around her wrist just in case — although she had no intention of falling asleep. She struggled to stay awake as Cameron drifted off. He was lying beside her on the soft ground, his eyes heavy.

There was something so peaceful, so calming about the forest with the sound of the splashing water and the birds clattering in the trees.

An hour later, she was still fighting sleep as a light rain began to mist her face. But the thought that Cameron might wake and somehow get away from her and might wander into the forest or fall into the stream was just enough to keep her eyes from closing.

She unfastened his reins from her wrist and set about tidying their things away, packing them into the base of the buggy. The wind had dropped. The birds were quieter and the only sound was the splashing water and . . .

She stood upright and listened. It sounded like a voice.

'Wake,' Cameron sprang upright. 'Wake!'

'I can see you're awake.' Anna laughed as she slipped him into his little rain jacket and wondered why she'd forgotten to bring her own. 'It's time for us to go home.'

'Home,' he echoed, liking the sound of that. There it was again. That voice. A call. Perhaps it was a fox. Or a bird. Anna suddenly felt very vulnerable and very much alone.

'Shoutin',' Cameron said as she made to put him in his buggy.

'You hear it, too?'

Anna set off in the direction of the voice. If she kept following, it would take her off the path, but as long as she was careful and took proper note of her surroundings, she could find her way back.

'Clever boy, Cameron,' she said. 'You were right.'

The trees seemed to thicken and while bracken and brambles tangled in her legs, thin twigs scratched her face and arms, but then they were on another path and the voice was closer still.

'Horse,' Cameron said. Anna turned and almost jumped out of her skin. The beautiful chestnut horse had been standing silent in the shadows of the trees. He was saddled and his reins hung down.

'Hello,' Anna said, approaching cautiously. The horse didn't seem at all bothered by her presence and allowed her to stroke him. 'Good boy. Where's your rider, eh?'

'Help me!'

'Hold on, I'm coming,' Anna called and hurried down an incline towards the voice. Just beyond an old fallen tree she saw a girl lying in a hollow.

She fumbled in her pocket for her mobile phone. The signal wasn't great, but at least she had one. The priority was to summon help, then she could assess the girl's injuries and relay them to the rescue team.

The first time she tried to make the call, the phone beeped at her and ended the call. Battery was good. She always made sure her battery was fully charged. The signal was intermittent though. She tried again.

★ ★ ★

Mac picked up his mobile phone when it rang for the fourth time. As before it rang just once, then the caller hung up. The caller ID was Anna. She must have a lousy signal wherever she was. He'd been wading through books and notes, trawling the internet and speaking to colleagues, but had found nothing to link Christa's illness with Anna. The only way Anna could have aplastic anaemia would be by a cruel and bizarre coincidence.

He called up Anna's number to return her call.

'Mac!' she yelled and the phone went dead. He knew from the tone of her voice that she was in trouble. He tried calling Anna again, but the answering service cut in. She was out of range. It had been a sheer fluke that he'd managed to speak to her at all.

Before setting out himself, Mac called Colin Harker. No one knew the forest better than him.

'I'll get some of the boys together to start a search,' Colin said at once.

Mac knew there was one way to get into the heart of the forest quickly.

He rushed outside and pulled open the workshop door. The bike was under a grey tarpaulin. He dragged the tarp off and flung it to one side. The bike had been fixed after the accident, but Mac had never ridden it since. Had vowed never to touch it again. He kept it as a reminder of how fragile his own life could be.

'Okay, you beast,' he murmured. 'You owe me!'

His crash helmet had been discarded after his accident, but he'd kept a spare and he pulled it down over his head, then straddled the bike. As he eased it out of the workshop onto the drive, he could feel the power of it, feel it wanting to race away.

'Not this time,' he muttered. 'This time we do it my way.'

He upped the revs, turned out onto the road then picked up speed.

10

'You must keep still,' Anna said to the girl who was writhing in the bracken. 'You may have a neck or spine injury that . . . '

It was no use. The girl was crying hysterically, pleading with Anna to help her to her feet, screaming that things were crawling on her. She was probably right about that, Anna thought as various nasty looking bugs landed on her own arms.

Anna tried to take hold of the girl's hands, but she was flailing about and caught Anna a sharp blow in the face almost knocking her off balance.

Cameron was distressed and began to cry, too, but Anna dare not move him from the harness on her back. There was nowhere safe to set him down and for now the safest place for him was exactly where he was.

He was screaming, the girl was screaming, Anna couldn't get through to either of them.

She remembered the whistle Mac had insisted she take with her. She blew into it. The sound was enough to break through the pandemonium.

The screaming and crying stopped. She stuffed the whistle in her pocket and smiled down at the girl.

'Can you tell me your name?'

'Camilla,' the girl croaked.

'I'm Anna and I'm a doctor. I know you're uncomfortable there, but it's vitally important that you keep as still as you can until help arrives.'

'I have things . . . crawling on me,' she whimpered. 'I don't like spiders.'

'They're not spiders, I promise,' Anna said. They were ants and while it was good news that Camilla could feel them moving about her body, it wasn't particularly pleasant for her. 'I'm going to look around to see if I can find something to help you keep your neck still. Don't worry if you can't see me,

I'll still be nearby.'

'Is help coming?'

'Yes,' Anna lied. She intended to try out her phone again as soon as she was a reasonable distance away from Camilla. As she straightened up, her back protested. Cameron was quite a weight.

She found two sturdy logs, and took them back to Camilla, placing one each side of her head.

'That will remind you not to move your head, okay?'

'My back hurts.' Camilla began to sob.

'What is your horse called?' Anna asked, trying to distract Camilla.

'Jazz,' Camilla's voice was strained.

'He's beautiful,' Anna said. 'I expect you ride a lot.'

'Yes,' Camilla said, her vocal chords loosening as she began to relax.

'Were you on your own today?'

'Yes,' Camilla whimpered. 'I'm not supposed to ride on my own in case . . . ' she broke off and bit hard on her lip.

'We all do things we shouldn't sometimes, Camilla,' Anna replied.

* ★ ★ ★

Mac almost lost the tail end of the bike as he turned off the road and onto the forest path. He responded by speeding up, kicking up dirt in his wake — this time he was not going to lose control. All manner of possibilities raged through his mind and he eased up the speed a little acutely aware that he must get there in one piece. Anna could be hurt — or little Cameron.

He slowed his speed for the bends, gritted his teeth and sped up on the straights praying a deer or fox wouldn't appear on the path before him. Rain started to fall, not the light gentle rain of earlier, but a downpour. He felt the ground turn greasy beneath his wheels, knew he had to exercise caution, knew that he had to find Anna soon.

At last he came to a clearing and could see something through the trees.

Cameron's buggy. Hope filled his heart until he realised it was abandoned.

He skidded to a halt, killed the engine and kicked back the stand. Yanking his helmet off he looked around, rain cascading down on him now, relentless and hard running in rivers down his face, plastering his hair to his head. He cupped his hands around his mouth and shouted.

★ ★ ★

Anna tried to make a canopy over Camilla, to stop the rain falling on her.

Then she heard it. The sound of a chainsaw. No, not a chainsaw. Something far more powerful.

'Hear that, Camilla?' she cried, fumbling in her pocket for the whistle, dragging it out, pressing it between her trembling lips. Rain ran down her face as she blasted on the whistle.

'Anna!' The voice came from so far away.

'Over here!' she yelled.

She could hear him now, his feet crunching through the undergrowth, his voice calling out to her, letting her know he was coming. Mac. Oh, Mac! Her legs went weak with relief and she almost fell as she gave one last blast on the whistle. He crashed through the trees, his strong arms thrusting branches aside until he stood before her, soaked to the skin, hair glued to his head and never having looked so gorgeous.

'Anna,' he cried, his face crumpling with relief. 'Oh, Anna, thank goodness! Cameron's with you. I thought . . . are you okay?'

He covered the distance between them and gathered her into his arms, holding her as if he'd never let her go. His hands finding the harness on her back and Cameron safely fastened into it.

'It's not me, Mac,' she said and he looked past her and saw the stricken girl for the first time. 'I've immobilised her as best I can.' She filled him in on what had happened.

'We're going to get you out of here,

Camilla,' Mac said softly. 'I'm going to have to ask you to be patient while I go and call an ambulance.'

'Are you okay?' He turned to Anna and held her upper arms.

She nodded but she felt far from okay. The world kept spinning.

'I think maybe you should sit down. It can't be easy standing with Cameron on your back. You all right, Cam?'

'Mac!' Cameron burst out. 'Hug! Down! Down!'

'Not right now,' Mac said. 'I have to go away to get a phone signal.'

'What was that?' Anna said, hearing the sound of more engines.

'Colin Harker to the rescue.' Mac grinned.

Mac's heart was in his mouth as he went back the way he'd come. In the clearing Colin appeared on a quad bike and took something from his pocket.

'Radio,' he said. 'Never mobile phones, this might be old-fashioned, but since Gavin's accident I've decided old technology is sometimes best. You get back to Anna and I'll get one of the boys to call an ambulance.'

Mac ran to where he'd left Anna. She looked as if she might collapse.

'Anna.' He ran to her, put his arms around her and held her tight.

'I feel so . . . ' she murmured. He unfastened the harness as her legs finally gave way and she sank to the ground. He scooped Cameron up in his arms.

'Don't worry,' he said. 'I've got him. You just sit there and rest.'

Anna smiled weakly and leaned against the sodden bark of a tree, closing her eyes. He looked down at her. She looked so ill, his heart contracted. Once this was over, he was going to have to have a serious talk with her. She opened her eyes and looked at him. She smiled and it tore at his heart.

★ ★ ★

'Watch your footing — it's very slippery just here,' Mac warned.

'Hey, Mac, would you rather do this yourself?' The paramedic laughed.

Mac grinned and took a step back, leaving them to do their job. Cameron was still in his arms, growing sleepy and getting heavier.

'Mac, let me,' Colin said, reaching out for the boy. 'Come on, laddie.'

Cameron was too sleepy to care who he was with. Colin opened his jacket and nestled Cameron inside.

'At least it's dry in there.' Colin laughed as Cameron pressed his thumb between his lips and closed his eyes. 'I'll get him back to Mary's. You'll be all right getting back under your own steam?' He looked pointedly at Anna who was asleep leaning against a tree. 'I wouldn't swear to it, Mac,' Colin said. 'But last time I looked we didn't have any Tsetse flies in the forest. Something's making that girl sleep though.'

'Yeah.' Mac chewed on his lip. 'I know.'

'And you call yourself a doctor.' Colin chuckled heartily and shook his head as he walked off. Mac watched him go — just what was so funny?

Anna woke and for a moment didn't know where she was. Then she realised she was leaning against something warm and soft. Mac. He was cradling her in his arms. He'd wrapped a jacket round her shoulders, too.

'Hey,' he said hoarsely.

She sat bolt upright and looked scared.

'Cameron's safe. Colin's taken him home and Mary will look after him. Camilla's on her way to hospital. It's you I'm concerned about now.'

'Me?' She got up, brushing wet leaves from her legs. 'I'm okay.'

'You are clearly not okay,' he said. 'You fell asleep sitting against a tree and you've been sleeping in your room at the surgery. I want to arrange some tests for you, Anna. Or have you already done that for yourself?'

'I want to go home,' she said, hurrying off, trying to run away from his questions. 'I want to get back to Cameron.'

'Well, you're heading the wrong way,

for a start,' he said calmly.

She stopped dead, spun around and marched back towards him.

'I know that,' she said defiantly.

'At least you have some colour in your cheeks now.'

'Are you laughing at me?'

'Wouldn't dream of it,' he said, but he was smiling. She began to walk the other way, heading towards a thick covering of bracken and brambles.

'Anna, where are you going?'

'Home,' she said, looking for a way through, tearing back branches with her hands. Surely this was the way Mac had come? 'To Cameron.'

'Cameron is fine,' Mac said. 'Stop charging at everything like a bull at a gate. You're way off the way out of here and you're going to get . . . stung,' he finished as she yelped and disappeared, falling into a bed of nettles.

He turned his back to her and wiggled his fingers.

'Come on,' he said, laughing. 'You know the drill by now.'

'Oh, really,' she said as she was lifted onto his back. 'This is ridiculous.'

'Shut up,' he said. 'Or I might be tempted to leave you here.'

She clamped her mouth shut.

'Our transport home,' he said, easing her down when they reached the clearing. She stood in front of him, looking up at him, her heart thudding.

'The bike? The one you were never going to ride again?'

'I only have one helmet. You'll wear that,' he ignored her question.

'No way. I'm not letting you ride that thing without a crash helmet.'

He put the helmet on her head and pulled the strap taut under her chin.

'I'll drive slowly,' he said.

She watched him swing his leg over the seat and she followed suit, getting on behind him. She'd never ridden on a motorbike in her life. Fastening her hands round his waist, she prepared to hang on for dear life as he started the machine and it roared into life beneath them.

Anna had gone from looking sickly and wan to looking the picture of health in moments — she looked positively radiant. So what was wrong with her? If she were a patient of his, he'd be getting her a pregnancy test.

'What is it?' she cried when he swerved a little.

'Nothing,' he said, remembering Colin's laughter. *Call yourself a doctor!*

Pregnant! Could she be? He'd assumed she was on the Pill, but by her own admission she steered clear of relationships and didn't she say she didn't believe in taking medication unnecessarily?

Blind fool. He slowed down.

'Can't you go any faster?' she said.

'I don't want to risk you falling off.'

That's why she was getting up nights. A lot of his pregnant mums complained of disturbed nights having to get up to go to the loo. And the tiredness. Extreme as it was, he'd seen it before and it would pass.

His baby. He could barely wipe the smile off his face. Was that why she wanted to run away? She wanted to keep this to herself? No, she wouldn't do that to him. There had to be another reason.

When they arrived back at the surgery, Hannah Harker was approaching, holding out a blanket, ready to wrap it around Anna.

'Your little one is safe at home with Mary. She's taken him for a nice warm bath and she said she'll see he gets something to eat.'

'Thanks,' Anna said. Another car pulled up and Martin jumped out.

'What's going on?' he said. 'Are you okay? Mac, you've not been on that thing again?' Concern? What a surprise. A pleasant one. This was a side to Martin that people rarely got to see. It was Hannah who explained while Martin listened, his face turning white.

'Yes, well you can come with me, Anna,' he said. 'I'll drive you home. What about you, Mac? Do you want a lift? Someone can pick up the bike.'

'Thanks, Martin, but I'll ride it

home.' Mac grinned at his cousin.

'You get that crash helmet on, Mac, and drive carefully,' Hannah said. 'Remember what happened last time you rode that wretched thing.'

He grinned and nodded and obediently put the helmet on.

'I'll get showered and changed and come down to see you, Anna,' he said. 'There's something I want to discuss with you urgently.'

Anna got into Martin's car prepared for his usual hostility.

'It would kill him if anything happened to you,' Martin said as they drove.

'What?'

'Okay, maybe not kill him.' Martin shrugged. 'But since you got here, he's been so happy. I wasn't sure about taking you on and I'm sorry about that. I was wrong. I was just worried for Mac — he's like a big brother and I didn't want to see him hurt again, but I think he'll be more hurt if you go.'

She turned away. This just got harder and harder.

11

Anna opened the door. She'd had a shower and now felt more human. Cameron was sound asleep, none the worse for his soaking in the forest, and Mary had gone to her annexe. Mac was standing outside, leaning against the porch, a casual smile slung across his face.

'It's good news?' Anna said. 'About Camilla?'

'Camilla?' he said distractedly. 'Oh, yes, it is. No spinal cord injury.'

Anna pulled the door open wider. Mac entered and looked around.

'I like what you've done in here. It's cosy. Feels like a real home.'

Yes. It does feel like a real home, Anna thought wistfully.

'What did you want to talk to me about, Mac?' Anna asked.

'I think you know the answer to that,' he said.

She sighed.

'I won't change my mind about resigning. I'll make some coffee.'

'Nice bruise on your face,' he said. 'How did it happen?'

'Camilla thumped me.' She laughed as his eyebrows rose in surprise. 'It was an accident. She was hysterical.'

She went to the kitchen and returned with two mugs of coffee. She placed the cup down on the table in front of him and as she made to move away to an armchair, he grasped her wrist and pulled her down beside him.

'I don't know what you're doing, Mac,' she said shakily, her resolve disastrously close to crumbling. 'But it won't work. And you should know I've changed my mind about leaving.' She hated herself for the way his face lit up. The relieved smile. The joy in his eyes.

'What I mean is I'm not going to wait,' she added quickly. 'It's too difficult. I want you to find a replacement for me as soon as possible.'

'That's really what you want?' he said

after a long, painful silence. 'And you still won't tell me why?'

'I can't, Mac,' she said, unable to hold his gaze any longer. It was just too painful looking at him, knowing what she was throwing away.

'You set a lot of store by the truth, Anna,' he said. 'So I'm telling you the truth now. I love you. I want to marry you. Now you look me in the eye and tell me in all honesty that you don't love me.'

'I . . . I can't,' she said, tears choking her. 'Don't make this harder than it already is, Mac. Just accept that I have a very good reason for leaving.'

'No, I won't.' He reached up, running his fingers through her hair. 'The rain has made your hair so soft.' He let it fall through his fingers. 'When you were lost in the forest, you called me. You didn't try to call the emergency services, you called me. Doesn't that tell you something, Anna?'

'You know the forest better than anyone,' she said weakly, knowing she hadn't even considered calling anyone else. 'It made sense to call you.'

'No, it didn't,' he said. 'You called me because you knew I'd find you, and if you leave here now, I will find you, I promise. I'll find you and bring you back and if you won't come back, then I'll stay with you wherever you are. If it means I won't lose you, Anna, I'll go to the ends of the earth with you.'

'Stop it!' she cried, pushing him away. 'Is this what you did to Abigail? You made her stay here? And then when you got fed up with her, you drove her away?'

'I didn't make Abi do anything against her will,' he said. 'I didn't stop her going to town, staying with her friends. I even put up with her affairs. She had it all her own way all the time except over one thing and that's why she left me, because I would not give her what she wanted.'

'And what exactly was it that she wanted?' Anna demanded.

'She wanted a baby,' Mac said

tersely. 'First it was a particular car, then it was a painting by a particular artist. She was constantly testing me and once I gave her what she wanted, she lost interest. I would love children, Anna. Nothing would make me happier than to fill my house with kids, to see it littered with toys, to have it ringing with the sound of happy childish voices. But to have a child on a whim?' He shook his head. 'No,' he said. 'I would not do that to a child and so she left me. Did you notice how quickly she tired of playing the dutiful niece to Hilda?'

'Poor Hilda,' Anna murmured.

'Don't pity her. There are plenty of people in this village that love her and she knows it. Abi was only interested in hanging around for as long as she thought Hilda might die and leave her some money.'

'That's harsh, Mac. She seemed so upset at the hospital,' Anna said.

'She's manipulative. She can turn tears on at will. She likes to soak up sympathy and I daresay you gave it to her.'

'And yet you want to give marriage another go — with me?' Anna said.

'You're not Abigail,' he said, reaching out for her again. 'You're Anna and I love you very, very much. I didn't want to have children with Abi, but that doesn't mean I don't want children or that I don't want our child.'

She caught her breath. Was he saying what she thought he was saying? He reached out and pressed his hand against her stomach. He knew.

'I wanted to marry you when I thought you might be ill and I still want to marry you now that I know you're not ill, but pregnant. Now tell me you don't love me, Anna. Tell me that and I promise I will leave you alone.'

She pressed her hand over his.

'I do love you, Mac,' she said. 'More than anyone else in my life. But you're taking on more than me, more than our baby — there's Cameron.'

'I love him, too,' Mac said, smiling. 'He's a part of you and he will be a part of our lives together. And I swear I will never let you down, any of you.'

'You have to be sure,' she persisted. And Mac took her in his arms, kissed her until she was dizzy and there was no room left for doubts in her mind. She wasn't taking a step into the unknown so much as leaping into a golden future with the man she adored.

She'd come home and she was going to stay.

THE END